PIT STOP: BABY

CRESCENT COVE BOOK 4

TARYN QUINN

This book is a work of fiction. The names, characters, places, and incidents are products of the writer's imagination or have been used fictitiously and are not to be construed as real. Any resemblance to persons, living or dead, actual events, locales or organizations is entirely coincidental.

Pit Stop: Baby

Rainbow Rage Publishing
ISBN: 978-1-940346-62-5

Cover by LateNite Designs
Photograph by Deposit Photos

First print edition: January 2020

You're cold and hot
You burn out like a match
Keep a slip knot in the strings you attach
You think it's easy, but that's a lie
The only reason that you're good at goodbye is
Every boy you ever met, was too easy to forget
Well, I ain't going out like that

MAKE YOU MISS ME, SAM HUNT

ONE

December (The night before my sister's wedding)

The cheers around me threatened my steady hand. That and maybe the hundred proof whiskey I'd been drinking all night like it was Diet Coke. I was here for a good time and that was what I was having.

Mostly.

Mopping up the floor with the third team of dart players didn't hurt. Or the extra seventy bucks in my ass pocket from the idiots betting against me.

When you lived in a small town like Turnbull, there wasn't much else to do but play darts and pool with the guys. Especially since I wasn't the type of girl to join a flock of women and preen at the bar. I liked to be in the middle of the action and knew I pissed off more women than I became friends with. I was the girl who excelled at darts but could run a table when needed.

"Come on, sweetheart, we don't have all night."

I ignored the guy with the two-pack-a-day voice. Justin? Jerry? I couldn't remember and didn't particularly care. He was just pissed because I'd trounced him first tonight. I'd taken twenty off of him before he even realized I'd won the round.

Judd, right. That was his name. Like the hot dude from *The Breakfast Club*. He even looked like him a little. Only it was the version of him on the wrong side of forty and didn't turn my crank. Not that I had a problem with guys heading for forty and beyond. I'd played trophy girlfriend a few times when I was in my early twenties.

The bling was alluring. Guys in their twenties couldn't afford sparklers like men with careers. The only problem there was I actually liked having a conversation with a guy. When you were from a different generation, it made things a little difficult. And I didn't have it in me to be shallow enough to just enjoy the rich guy ride.

"Come on, Ryan, I just want a chance to win back my money."

"My name is Rylee." I flicked my dark hair over my shoulder and lifted my lucky purple dart.

No do-overs. One and done only for this girl. Getting fired three weeks before Christmas made a girl grab some perspective.

It was time to finish this damn game. I'd been stringing it out with the guys around me calling out their own numbers in the game of 301. Each time I aced the shot, I picked up another five bucks.

But if I had to listen to Billy Joel's "Piano Man" come belting out of that jukebox one more time tonight, I would eject the ancient record with my boot.

I blew out a slow breath and hit the center of the triple ring. Six guys groaned. "I believe that's the final sixty points I needed?" I turned, downed my shot. I made gimme fingers and they each dropped a twenty on the table. I swiped up the pile. "Pleasure playing with you guys."

"Bet you can't hit a double bullseye in three rapid shots."

The voice was deep. It carried from the back of the pack of men. The fact that my nipples instantly hardened and tried to bust through my glittery baby doll shirt made me swallow my acidic reply.

Maybe not so bored anymore.

"Another round for the table, darlin'." The voice was smooth caramel over chocolate lava cake.

"You got it."

Our waitress's voice went breathy. At least that was a good sign that Mr. Caramel's voice might in fact have a matching face.

Not that I cared. Much. My current jobless status meant I'd take his money regardless.

I twirled my dart through my fingers. "What's the bet?" I had a cool two hundred in my pocket. Enough to cover groceries for a month. If I could double that, it would be even better.

The guy came out of the shadows and my nipples weren't the only thing at attention. My clit and heart did a double tap like I was at the top of a rollercoaster one click past the drop.

Hello, caramel.

He matched the word in every way. Dark blond hair cut close, along with a scruffy face that was just beyond sandpaper to that perfect buzz that could make the very best friction when used correctly.

His smirk told me he was aware of his appeal. It remained to be seen if the smirk came with a boatload of asshole or charm.

But it was the eyes that had me sunk. Barrel-aged whiskey—my favorite. Even in the dim bar, they glowed hot and interested.

Did I mention my clit was doing a salsa beat? No? It sure was.

Unfortunately, I had just enough of said barrel-aged whiskey in my system to drown out self-preservation.

"What do you have in that perfect ass pocket?"

I grinned up at him. "Three hundred."

Lies. But if I could take him for a little more…

He glanced around at the men who were suddenly finding their boots very interesting. "Is that right? Then obviously you are needing a bit of a trouncing."

I turned back to the board. "So, that's a bet then?"

"Don't want to shake on it?" His voice came from right behind me. Far too close.

But remember that little mention about too much whiskey? Yeah, tequila had nothing on whiskey when it came to me.

I turned until we were almost lined up. I nibbled on my lower lip as I stared at his full, mack-worthy mouth. There was something about a man who had full lips. No teeth mashing would be a part of our future.

Because I was going to taste that mouth if it was the last thing I did tonight.

I locked my gaze with his. "Sure, we can seal the deal." I rested my hand on his chest and went up on my toes.

His eyes went wide with surprise as I gripped the deceptively gorgeous cashmere of his sweater. Not exactly the kind of guy who belonged in a dive bar. I yanked him down and covered his mouth in a quick, hot kiss.

I was expecting a little buzz, but not *this.* Not the urge to drag him down closer. Usually, I was more talk than action when it came to men. I enjoyed flirting and could spin it out for ages without it ever coming to anything.

This fried my plans and my circuits like a…

Hmm. I didn't really have a likeness in my electrified brain. And it was not because of the whiskey.

He rocked back on his heels, but not before his long fingers slid along my lower back. His fingers were not as soft as the sweater, which made him all the more intriguing. I'd been expecting paper-pusher hands. "Not exactly what I had in mind."

"It's a big bet." I stepped away and turned back to the board. My fingers trembled a little. Damn, that probably hadn't been my best move. "What was the shot?"

"Don't remember?"

Nope. I sure didn't. "Thought it might have been too easy but didn't want to make life harder for myself if I didn't have to."

"Double bullseye within three quick throws."

I tipped my head with a slow smile. "Do you do everything quick?"

His low laugh made all the things jangle inside me. "Loaded question."

"If you have to think about it too much, then I probably don't want to know." I picked up my lucky dart with two of the others on the table. I straightened my shoulders and got into position.

I shot off the first two, and a light, warm breeze floated by my ear a la Kevin Costner's *Robin Hood*. The third nailed the rim of one of the wires and clattered to the floor. My lucky fucking purple dart.

I whirled on him, my hands on my hips. "What the fuck?"

"We didn't establish any rules." A slow smile transformed his handsome face into downright sinful.

"That's bullshit." I resisted the urge to stomp my boot, but only barely.

He twirled me around and cozied up behind me. I stiffened in his arms, but he pointed to the board. "You still won there, Artemis."

Startled, I twisted to look up at him. Mythology? Wears hot cashmere sweater, has man hands, and smart. I'm not sure where this trifecta came from, but I was afraid to blink. He'd totally be a figment of my buzzy imagination.

His stubbled cheek brushed along mine. "Guess I owe you three hundred, my little huntress."

"From Artemis to huntress? I'm not sure I want to be downgraded."

"I was thinking more like Princess Diana."

I laughed. "Now a super blond and definitely not alive version. At least you could let me be Megan or something."

"More like Wonder Woman." He flicked his finger along my wavy dark hair. "You're hot and fierce like her."

"Oh." I swallowed. Yeah, I could definitely deal with that comparison. "I definitely don't have her boobs."

I slammed my eyes shut. *Good going, Rylee.*

His hand spanned my waist. "Your breasts are perfect." He nipped my ear. "You started this little dance, but are you willing to finish it?"

The guys around us had dissipated when they were no longer part of the fun. They'd taken their free beers and gone about their business. I was alone with him. Well, as alone as I could be in a bar still half-full of people.

My breath died in my chest. Did I really have the balls to take him up on his offer? I'd done this before, both times ending in disaster. A college hookup the one and only year I'd attended. He'd been all talk and barely a two-pump chump.

The other had been a temp job with a fiery end. That was more hate fuck with a side of stupidity. Also, more amazing in theory than in execution. I'd only ended up with bruises on my ass from the desk and no orgasms to be had.

"I'm sorry, huntress. I didn't mean to overstep." He took a step back.

Obviously, I'd taken too long to answer. Lost in the morass of the many mistakes in my past, I'd given him the wrong sign. Or maybe it was him moving back that gave me the courage to turn around and grab his hand. "One night. No repeats."

He turned back to me. "No repeats? Not even tonight?"

I swallowed. Could a guy actually go more than once without passing out? I'd thought that was just in books and movies.

I lifted my chin. "As many times as you can fit in one night, handsome."

He opened his mouth. I went up on my toes again and shut it for him.

I didn't want to know his name. I didn't want anything but a crazy night that would make this shitstorm of a week better. I had to stand up with my sister tomorrow and make everyone think I wasn't the world's worst fuck-up.

Again.

If I was going to make a crazy mistake, at least this guy seemed like he might make it worth the trouble.

Either way, I was about to find out.

TWO

March

ALL THAT MATTERED WAS DOING MY JOB WELL.

I had to make coffee. Everyone at work had an order and I had to get them right.

New girl.

Had to make a good impression.

Cream and sugar with a splash of caramel for Kathy. The good caramel. The kind that was kept behind the counter.

I fumbled across the counter. Not caramel. Not the good stuff.

Kathy would be mad.

Where was the caramel?

But what about Monty's coffee cake?

I moved to the shelves along the side and took a plate. Mustn't forget the cake. Caramel on the cake? Maybe he'd like that too. Where was the caramel?

"What the hell are you doing in my fucking café?"

I turned toward the sound. "I'm looking for caramel of course." I took the plate to the counter. "Monty wants coffee cake."

"Are you drunk?"

"No, it's morning. I don't drink in the morning." I moved back to the counter and took the lid off the muffin plate. No, he wanted coffee cake. "Okay, maybe I used to drink in the morning, but not anymore. I have to get coffee for work. Please don't make me late. Sam wouldn't like if I'm late. I'm the new girl, and I can't be late."

A bright light dented the fog.

"It's three in the goddamn morning. I don't have time to deal with this shit. You need to keep your damn edibles on the shelf unless you're sharing with friends."

"Edibles?" I frowned and looked down at the plate in my hand. I frowned. That wasn't my plate.

"Look what you did to my place."

The slam of a drawer made me stagger back a step. This was not my apartment. "Oh, God." I swayed a little and shook my head. Where the hell was I? "Oh, shit."

"I'm calling the cops."

"Wait!" I shook off the fog of sleep and confusion and slipped on sugar and coffee grinds. I barely caught myself on the counter. "Wait. Oh, God. I wanna die."

Macy Devereaux stood at the edge of the café with a baseball bat over her shoulder, dark hair in a messy braid, and her icy eyes dead serious. "What the hell are you doing in here?"

I closed my eyes, pushing my frazzled hair out of my face. "You won't believe me."

I didn't believe me. I couldn't believe this was happening.

Not again.

The particulars were fuzzy as they almost always were after one of my episodes—a lot of times I didn't remember much at all—but the signs were quite clear.

I glanced around at the huge mess on the floor and the counters. How the hell did I get into the café?

"You need to do some explaining or you'll be doing it with Sheriff Brooks."

"No, no. I'll clean it up. I'm so sorry."

"You're damn right you'll be cleaning it up. How the hell did you get in here? Don't make me ask again."

"I, um, don't know."

"What?" She lowered the bat. "What do you mean you don't freaking know? I have a security panel, for God's sake."

"4344."

Macy's eyebrows shot up. "You know the passcode?"

"I don't know how I know that. I can do this weird thing with tones though. If I ever heard it, I'd just know. From all my temp jobs on the phones. I've come down when you were opening up a few times."

Macy sighed and crossed the room to a closet. She left the bat there and came back with a broom. "Yeah, you harass me for coffee. This goes above and beyond."

I scrubbed my palm down my bare leg. Oh, great. *Please don't be half naked.* What did I wear to bed? I looked down and blew out a breath. At least I was wearing shorts.

I'd been so damn hot at night lately that I went to sleep wearing only a T-shirt half the time.

She held out the broom to me with an expectant nod.

After taking it, I looked down at my footprints ghosted through the scattered coffee and sugar. I lifted a foot and brushed it off with a wince. "So, I sleepwalk."

"Pardon?"

I swept up the granules into piles. Man, just how fine had I ground the freaking coffee? It was practically powder. "I used to do it a lot, but I grew out of it."

"I'm gonna say it's back. You know how many times you've done this?"

I winced. "More than once, I gather?"

"This would be the third time. Maybe fourth. The first time, I was totally freaked out. Thought I was losing my damn mind." She grabbed a rag and spray bottle from under the register. "Just had two plates with bagels sitting on the counter one morning last week."

"Oh, boy." Things had been moved around in my apartment, but I hadn't unpacked everything yet. I couldn't be sure if I stopped unpacking mid-box or if I'd just forgotten where I'd put things.

Like two plates with my bakery goods.

Evidently, Denialsville was a place I called home. I didn't want to believe it could be happening again. With the move, a new job, and having my sister so close to me that she was in my business all the time...

Yeah, stress was my first, middle, and last name.

"Then I came in to find a sugar bag open on the floor with sugar everywhere. So, then I thought I had a rodent problem. Unless it's a bat, I'm not interested in that kind of crap in my place."

"I'm so sorry. I swear, I didn't know."

Though wow, she liked bats? That was...different.

"The last time was coffee and caramel."

"Kathy loves your caramel." I pushed my crazy hair out of my face at Macy's deadpan expression. "I get coffee for the floral shop."

"Right. Black with two raw sugars, coffee regular with caramel, and double espresso shot mocha latte."

I blushed. "Yeah, that's us."

"So, you make coffee too, Houdini?"

I winced. "Worked at a coffee shop in high school."

"Not neatly."

"Yeah, well, you should have seen my kitchen when I was a teenager. I'd leave the door to the fridge open and put peanut butter-covered knives back in the drawer."

"You're a real peach."

My neck heated and I seriously wanted to run back up the stairs. "I used to do it a lot when I was in high school. Hormones and stuff, I guess." I used the back of my hand to push my hair back. I felt sticky and gross. "Can I wash up a bit?"

"Sure." Macy pointed at the boxes under the counter. "I was having cameras put in next week."

I ran the taps and soaped up my hands, digging out coffee grounds from under my nails. "How did you know I was in here? Did you hear me or something?"

"No. I set a nanny cam up until Gideon can put those in."

I looked around. "Where?"

She pointed to a bat tacked up with its wings extended in the corner of her display case. "Little camera in there. It has a motion sensor, but you can't see shit at night. All I saw was someone moving around in the dark."

"And you came down here with a baseball bat? Are you crazy?"

Macy tipped her head. "Really?"

"Well, you didn't know if I was a thief. You should have called the cops."

"You asked me not to call the cops."

"Well, of course, I don't want to get into trouble, but oh my God, what if I was dangerous?"

"Yeah, you and your sugar problem. Totally dangerous."

"I mean, I don't know you, really, but dude, not cool."

"I can take care of myself, don't worry." She dragged the garbage over and scraped my mess into the bag.

"I'll pay for it."

"For what?"

"The stuff I wasted."

Macy shrugged. "It's fine. Vee makes a bigger mess just walking through the back room."

"But I totally broke in and wrecked the place."

"Look, Rylee, right?"

I sighed. "Yeah, Rylee."

We'd spoken a few times, but Macy wasn't exactly the chatty type. And I was completely fine with that, other than the fact that I'd totally broken into her place. What in the fuck? How was this my life?

"I mean, we gotta figure out how to stop you from sleepwalking into my joint, but I'm not going to be a shit about it. It's not your fault or whatever. It's a condition." She flipped the end of her braid over her shoulder. "It's fine."

I tried to stop a smile. Macy was gruff. The only reason I kept coming back to her coffee shop was because she made the best coffee I'd ever tasted. Good thing, because she barked at her customers more than she smiled. And yet Brewed Awakening was busy all the time because she was a damn genius at coming up with the perfect combinations based on the person, not just a menu like most places.

"It usually comes up when I'm stressed. Evidently, moving and starting a new job is way more stressful than I thought it would be." The last time it had happened, I'd lost a boyfriend over it. And my current level of exhaustion should have been a freaking clue. That and the fact that my pants were getting a little tight.

The worst part of sleepwalking for me had always been the middle of the night eating. Diet all you want, but if your subconscious is trashing your diet, it ain't gonna work. Not that I was a hardcore dieter, but a carb sabotage sucked.

"Good thing it doesn't work like that for me. I'd be sleepwalking all over friggin' town."

I laughed. It was the only thing I could do. I was so far past embarrassed, I was in the next county. "Could you maybe…keep this between us?" I piled up plates from where I'd demolished her stacks. Luckily, they were plastic.

She gave me a sidelong glance. "It's damn good blackmail material."

My breath stalled.

"I'm kidding." She lobbed a towel at me.

I caught it and laughed. "Freaks some people out."

"Don't worry. I won't say anything. Nobody's fucking business anyway. Freaking small town busybodies don't need any other fodder."

I laughed. "I'm quite happy not to be part of that club."

"Give it time, Houdini."

We finished cleaning up in the quiet. The café really was peaceful without the bustle of people shouting orders behind the counter.

Macy's perpetual Halloween aesthetic had seemed weird when I first moved in, but now it just was. She had a wall of cubicle-style shelves, each decorated with a different type of scene. The overwhelming horror and fall elements made me smile.

I shifted a mug with the *Scream* Ghostface mask on it. "You a slasher flick fan?"

"Hell, yes."

I laughed. "I think I've seen every movie you have showcased in here."

"Oh, that's just for the regular people. The bottom two shelves are for the true aficionados."

I crouched and laughed at the woman wearing a machine gun for a leg. "No freaking way." I turned toward Macy standing behind me. "*Grindhouse?*"

"Girl, sometimes you just want to watch a girl blow some shit up without any of that politically correct bullshit."

"None of that in those movies for sure. God, they're so deliciously bad."

"You like them?" She cocked her hip with her arms folded over her chest. "Now I'm doubly glad I didn't call the cops."

I grinned up at her. "Me too." I tugged down my baby doll sleeping shirt. "I'm really sorry. I can't tell you how sorry."

Macy waved me off. "Forget it. No real harm done. Now that I don't think I'm losing my mind, or that zombies are infiltrating my café at night."

I laughed. "Well, my mom says I look a little zombie-like when I do the sleepwalking thing."

"It is a little freaky on the video I have. You kinda shuffle along like you're confused, but still have a destination in mind."

"Ugh. That sounds about right. The worst part is the insomnia that comes with it. I could stare at the ceiling for hours. Rain apps, thunderstorms—"

"White noise app," Macy interrupted.

"You know the drill then?"

"Girl, I haven't slept correctly since…ever. Why do you think I invent ways to caffeinate?"

"And I live for your lattes. Only way I get through the day."

"However, I do have a fairly cool way to chill out."

"Those edibles you mentioned?"

She snorted. "No, those just made me even more anxious and panicked. Pass times eleven, thanks."

I sighed. "Me too."

"Sucks." She crossed to a little end table by the couch along the wall. "However..." She plucked a little remote out of a hidden panel on the side of the table. "I do have this." She pushed the button and a huge screen lowered from the ceiling.

"Oh my God. That is glorious."

The screen filled with dozens of movies from her collection in iTunes. "I've got anything you could think of for movies."

"Got *Scream* in there?"

She paged ahead. "Of course I do."

"Now the real question. Popcorn?"

"Caramel and cheddar."

My smile spread. "Oh, we're going to be very good friends."

"I'll get the popcorn and hot chocolate."

I dropped onto the couch. Tonight could have gone very badly, but somehow I'd backed into finding a new friend. It almost made up for the very terrifying realization that I had to deal with sleepwalking again.

Just freaking awesome.

THREE

Being a family man was for the birds. Whatever the fuck that actually meant.

I wasn't quite sure what had possessed my brother Dare to go from one small town to an even more bucolic one, but then again, here I was visiting for the second time in a handful of months. The last time I'd been home before that had been…well, years ago.

The racing circuit was a very exacting mistress. She demanded all my time and I'd been more than happy to follow her from town to town. The lure of the track and the power of the cars had always fired my blood. Even before my brother had left the NASCAR pro-circuit, I'd been angling for a way to get my name up on the leaderboard.

It had been slightly easier with Dare out of the picture. He'd been a rising star with more natural aptitude than anyone else driving at the time. How many drivers could race their way up the ranks into the top ten within a year?

Not many. But he had. And I'd longed to do the same.

When he left to start a family, I'd been happy to step up and show everyone that I wasn't just Dare Kramer's little brother. I'd been shocked that he would give everything up for a kid and that shrew of a woman he'd gotten together with, but that was Dare. Ever the responsible one. Even when he'd been working in the pit crews, he'd been sought after as the singular mechanic to have on your team. But his blinding loyalty had kept him from climbing out of the rookie ranks.

And now he was here in Crescent Cove at a mechanic shop doing fucking oil changes instead of working on the crankiest engines on the planet.

I couldn't be that guy. Not ever.

Oh, because you're so happy?

I ignored the voice. I'd been actively avoiding it since I'd left Nashville. I had three different sponsor contracts sitting in my email inbox right now. My agent was blowing up my phone every other hour asking what the hell I was waiting for.

My last sponsor had decided against doing another year on the pro-circuit. Instead of freaking out like my entire pit crew, I'd felt nothing but relief. My usual crew had scattered to the four winds to other teams within a week. Not a single one of them had even bothered to ask me if I was moving on to another team. They'd just hit the road.

And that was the life. Ever changing when it came to pit crews and sponsors, even the cars.

Me? I'd just been driving for pleasure for the first time in nearly ten years.

I'd driven out to California and took the time to actually enjoy the coastal highway instead of flying over it between races. The motor on my Camaro had shit the bed halfway across Colorado. That was pretty much when I decided my cross-country escapade was over.

Driving solo wasn't all it was cracked up to be.

In more ways than one.

So, here I was back in Crescent Cove. No crew, no stock car, and no real idea what the hell I wanted to do with myself. I could take a year off and try to get back into the game. I'd have to practically start over to gain traction again, and part of that was appealing.

Everything seemed too easy, too boring right now. My life was literally built around a stopwatch and driving in circles. Once, it had meant everything to me and I wasn't sure when that started to change.

The day a huntress made you beg.

I tightened my fingers around the steering wheel of my rental. Dark hair, dark eyes, and a laugh that stayed with me months later.

Of course that laugh came out of a mouth I couldn't forget for a number of other reasons.

Fuck, I couldn't go there right now. The last thing I needed was to walk around town with a hard-on.

I found a parking spot across from the park. And there was the big old gazebo my brother had gotten married in.

I'd never seen him happier. Maybe it had been then that I'd felt the first twinge of dissatisfaction with my life.

The handwriting had been on the wall even before that. Instead of the stag party I'd been trying to put together for Dare, we ended up at The Spinning Wheel. Dare hadn't been interested in partying the night away. He'd barely grunted his way through a beer with four—oh, yeah, partying it up hard—of his friends before making excuses to go home to his kid.

And sure, Wes was damn cute, but it wasn't like I was in town all that damn often. Was I completely out of Dare's life at this point?

Yep. That's affirmative.

I slammed the door on that thought and wandered down the wet sidewalks toward the pier. Spring in upstate New York was in full effect. Rain, rain, oh, and more rain. The lake was choppy with the leftover wind from the last storm that had followed me up from the city.

The last time I'd been here, the entire town had been decked out in its Christmas finery. Now there was mud and slivers of snow clinging to the edges of the grass determined to break through.

The gray sky fit my mood though. As did the sun trying to burn its way through the misty clouds. I was tired of the sameness in my life. Trials, tryouts, speed tests, and safety checks had ruled every moment of my day. Then the nights had been about going to bars just to ease the loneliness.

The night before Dare's wedding had been far more interesting than any other for a damn long time. A woman who didn't want strings or do-overs. It should have been the perfect way to spend a night.

And it had been.

The problem was it had left me wanting more.

Watching my little huntress stomp up to me in her midnight dress with her witchy dark eyes flashing outrage had lit me up like a high-octane fuel cocktail. Christ, she was amazing.

And now she was my sister-in-law.

Just my fucking luck.

The blare of a horn made me turn toward the road. A boat of a Cadillac was turning on to Main Street. Pure white with the turn radius of a damn semi. I didn't even know anyone who drove one of those anymore. Just the bloated, ugly versions that were on the showroom floors now.

New cars were computers with wheels. They had no soul.

I headed back down the pier to the sidewalk and passed the bank, which seemed unnaturally large for such a small town. Then again, if I remembered correctly, it had been decked out for Christmas like it was Park Avenue in New York City. The whole town took on a Hallmark Channel kind of aura.

Even now in the gray, muddy days before spring officially sprung, Main Street in Crescent Cove was like a damn postcard. The storefronts were neatly swept, and trash didn't dare mar the sidewalk.

I ducked into a small coffee shop with virtually no business. A sign was up behind the counter that they were changing from selling java to a wine bar.

Man, even in small town USA, wine was getting popular.

I smiled at the girl behind the counter. "Wine bar, huh?"

"Yes. We started working with a vineyard not far from here to get some local wines in. Hoping to expand as we go. We can't compete with Brewed Awakening anyway, so we decided to change it up."

"Great idea." I glanced out the window. Across the street, there was a café with a line almost out the door. "Glad you're still doing coffee today. Looks serious over there."

"It's always like that." The pretty blond leaned forward and pitched her voice low. "Even I go over there for coffee."

"Well, I'll chance it. Medium dark roast, please."

"You got it." She turned away to the coffee canisters on the counter against the wall. I wandered to the large picture window and realized my brother's garage was right next to the bustling café. I'd walked right on by without giving it a thought.

"Here you are, sir."

I turned and smiled at the girl. "Thanks. Hey, I have to go see my mom. Any flower shops around here?"

"Actually, yes, just a few doors down."

I paid for my coffee and tucked an extra five bucks in her tip jar. "Thanks."

Her eyes brightened. "No, thank you."

"Good luck with the wine bar. Though you don't look old enough to sell."

She played with the strings of her apron. "I'll be twenty-one next month."

Christ, my bones just ached at the thought of being twenty-one again. Then again, being crammed in a car without a fucking door would do that. "Happy early birthday, darlin'."

"Thanks." She lowered her lashes and did that peering through them thing that chicks learned at age four.

I lifted my coffee in a salute. "Have a good one." I knew that look and before she asked for my number or passed me hers, I needed to get the hell out.

Luckily, she was probably too young to recognize me. NASCAR wasn't exactly huge in the area, but I never knew when a fan would come out of the woodwork.

I took a right out of the little shop, and sure enough, just around the bend a sidewalk chalkboard sign had bouquet specials listed. I sipped my coffee as I checked out the spreads in the window, then choked at the familiar woman arranging daisies and some other fluffy red flower in a basket.

My heart flipped around in my chest as if I was coming up on the damn checkered flag in the final lap. What the hell was *she* doing here?

Before I could think twice, I pushed through the door. A bell that could be in one of those damn Hallmark movies tinkled above my head. She didn't even look up. But a pretty older woman came around a half wall.

"Hello." Her face crinkled up into a friendly smile.

I smiled at her but nodded at my intended target. "I see someone I know."

"Oh." Her smile faltered a little. "We don't really do social calls during work hours."

My eyebrow zinged up. *Social call?* I widened my smile, adding a little charm. "She's my sister-in-law."

"Oh. You're related to Dare, aren't you?"

"Guilty."

Her eyes went big and she nibbled on her lower lip. "That race car driver."

My *oh, shit* antennae went a little twitchy, but I nodded. "That's me."

"You were all the town could talk about after the wedding."

"I bet."

The woman had the good grace to blush. "Yes, well it was quite…exciting."

That was one word for my first official interaction with Rylee Ford. Her screaming at me under a gazebo full of lights with half the town in attendance for my brother's wedding wasn't likely to be forgotten anytime soon.

Not by me either.

She was the one who'd wanted no names, no do-overs, nothing but one night. Too bad she couldn't always have what she wanted.

But maybe I was about to get a second chance when it came to my wants.

We'd just see.

I lifted my finger to my lips and strolled over to where Rylee was bopping her head to some internal beat. Or to the wireless earbuds she was wearing. She moved her hips in a soft sway that I remembered all too well. Okay, so maybe it had been more of an undulating rhythm as she rode me blind.

Thankfully, I was wearing a button-down shirt with the tails over my jeans to hide just how well I remembered that night in December.

I tapped her shoulder.

She jumped and swung around with the shears in her hand pointing out.

Only my quick reflexes saved my shirt. I jumped back. "Whoa."

She tugged out her earbud and pocketed it, then came two more steps toward me with the shears still in hand. "What are you doing here?"

"Nice to see you too, Ry."

"Rylee." The blond woman's gasp made Rylee take two steps back.

"Sorry. He scared me." She dropped the wicked-looking scissors and pasted on a fake smile. "Nice to see you again, Gage."

"I don't really believe you." I glanced at the blond, whose gaze was bouncing eagerly between us. I'd run far and fast from that invasive gossipy, glee-filled smile. I didn't know this woman, but I'd known plenty like her growing up.

My parents had a pizza place here in Crescent Cove, but they'd opened that after I left home. My original hometown of Laurel was similar, if a little more rundown than this homespun place. But they were all the same under the charm.

"Think I could steal Rylee for lunch?"

"It's not time—"

"Sure. It's slow right now."

Rylee pressed her lips together. I remembered her doing that in the bar just before she blew my damn mind with a kiss.

Somehow I didn't think I was going to be that lucky today.

"But I have to finish the baskets for the Perkins party." Rylee didn't sound petulant, but it was a close thing.

Since pissing her off was my favorite thing to do, I grinned at the older woman. "Thirty minutes won't matter much."

Rylee huffed out a breath. "You don't need to listen to him, Kathy."

"It's not every day that family is in town, right?"

"No. Definitely not." I smirked at Rylee. "We should definitely catch up."

I turned back to Kathy. "I'd love a big, sunny arrangement for my mother. You know, the kind to brighten her spirits on a gray day."

"Oh, that's lovely. Isn't that sweet, Rylee?" Kathy hurried around the counter for a little pad.

"Super sweet." Her voice was deadpan, and I had to strangle a laugh.

"I'll write that up and do that myself. I'll have it ready when you guys come back from lunch." Kathy gave me a sunny smile. "I'm assuming money is no object?"

Oh, I was going to pay for this one. "Not when it when it comes to my mom."

"Wonderful. Now you two have a nice lunch to catch up."

Rylee pulled out her other earbud and jammed it into the case in her pocket. "Oh, we will." She stepped over to where she'd been working and picked up a massive bag off the floor. She hooked it over her shoulder and headed for the door without another word.

"She missed me, I can tell."

Kathy tapped her pencil against her palm. "So I see."

I slipped through the door with a grin. Man, I hadn't realized how much I'd missed this woman until I saw her again.

Now I just had to remind her she'd missed me too.

FOUR

"I CAN'T BELIEVE YOU DID THAT." I STALKED DOWN THE SIDEWALK toward Brewed Awakening. I definitely hadn't had enough coffee to deal with Gage Kramer.

"Did what? Ask you to lunch?" he called from behind me.

"In a high-handed, dirty, and underhanded way."

"So, I'm high-handed and underhanded?"

His stupidly long legs had him catching up to me in like two long strides. Ugh. "Don't be an ass."

"Just making sure which it is." He grinned down at me.

"What are you doing here?"

"Aww, did you miss me, huntress?"

I scrunched up my shoulders. "Don't call me that." I did not need to remember him calling me that. Especially when he did it while I was...

Nope.

No.

Not going to think about that night.

"You liked it that—"

I whirled on him in the middle of the street. "We are not discussing that night. One and done, remember?"

"Just because it was one and done doesn't mean I don't remember every damn detail."

The laughter was no longer in his golden-brown eyes. Just the intensity I remembered so very vividly when he'd laced our fingers together over my head, pinning me to the sumptuous mattress at the Sherman Inn. He'd stretched me out and covered every inch of my body with his.

"You remember it too."

I swallowed. "It was good for a one-night stand." I whirled away from him and practically ran for the café.

Macy represented safety. One steely look from her and out of control hormones locked themselves down out of self-preservation.

"Oh, honey, if all one-night stands were like that, everyone would do them. You know it was more than that."

I shut my eyes as I braced myself on the wide double doors of Brewed Awakening. I shook off his words and swung open the door to the noise and craziness that was Macy's café. Dozens of people littered tables and lined up for coffee and food, and Macy's crew of people rushed around as orders were shouted. It was too noisy to talk to him.

Dear God, I needed coffee to handle this.

What the hell was he doing in town? He should be practicing driving or something. Whatever it was that race car drivers did between races. I didn't freaking know.

He followed me inside. I could feel his warmth behind me. Before Gage, no man had ever made me so aware of him in my space. The few guys I'd dated were fun. They were good guys who knew about boundaries and manners.

Gage knew about none of those things.

The tips of his fingers rested on my lower back, and I had to resist the urge to shiver followed directly by a lean in. Since the moment we'd met, we'd been invading each other's space. For God's sake, I'd kissed him before even attempting to know his name. That wasn't me. I might not want strings when it came to men, but at least there were names exchanged before my panties hung off the chandelier.

Not that *that* had occurred with Gage. It had actually been a Tiffany lamp, but close enough.

He lowered his mouth to my ear. "What's good here?"

I stepped away from him. "Everything."

His low laugh made me pick up the pace to get into line. I didn't need him making fun of me on top of it. In fact, I didn't need any of this. I was just getting settled in Crescent Cove. I had a decent job and I'd even made a new friend.

Sort of.

If late night break-ins and a love of scary movies counted anyway.

"Hey, mocha latte. How's it hanging?"

"I need a double shot."

Macy wiped down the counter. "And for your friend?"

Gage stepped up right behind me. I elbowed him back a step. The bastard just laughed. "Surprise me. I'm told you're a bit of a genius knowing what people need."

Macy glanced at me then at Gage. "Uh-huh. You got it." She tipped her head. "What do you do, stretch?"

"He's a race car driver."

"Ex-race car driver."

I spun around. "Excuse me?"

"You don't know...well, anything about me, huntress."

"Well, alrighty then." Macy looked between us then hurried away from us to her espresso machine.

I frowned up at him. "What does that mean?"

He shrugged. "You just made it way more interesting to be back in town."

"Wait, what?"

He leaned down into my space. "I was only passing through. Visit the folks, harass my brother. You know how it goes. Now? Well, Crescent Cove just got a lot more intriguing."

I was officially fucked, minus the orgasm. At least a recent one. And orgasms were not like pennies in the bank. Saving them up did not pay dividends. It just made you that much more likely to jump the first sexy dude who touched your…dart.

"Here you go." Macy rattled off the total for our drinks.

Gage held out his credit card. "Can you add two lunch specials to that?"

"Sure." She tapped her long finger along the edge of Gage's card. "All good, mocha?"

"What?" I blinked. God, I felt so dumb. I literally couldn't get past the part about him staying in town. "Oh, umm." I blinked up at the menu board with the lunch special of soup and grilled cheese. Sounded amazing actually. Even if my stupid body temperature would skyrocket for the rest of the day. "Yes, thank you."

Macy swiped his card and handed him his receipt.

Gage took it and stuffed a bill into the tip jar. "Thanks."

I didn't want to look, but fucking sue me. How he tipped said a lot about a guy. Twenty fucking bucks? Yeah, either he was trying to impress me—working—or he was throwing around money to look cool—asshole.

Jury was still out.

He took our cups with a charming smile for Macy. "Thanks." He turned, invading my space again. "Sit outside or in here?"

Considering it had been raining since I moved to town, I was taking the outdoors option. That and I could walk away faster if need be. "Outside." That, and I was already feeling a hot flash coming on. They were getting freaking ridiculous.

"I'll have Vee bring your food out."

"Thanks, Mace."

She simply nodded in her no-nonsense style and went on to the next customer.

It took some doing to get out of the café. I swore everyone in town must have been there for lunch though it was barely noon.

He gestured to a table at the edge of the outdoor patio.

I rushed over to grab it. Not because I wanted to get space between us. Surely not.

I'd barely slid my butt into a chair before a woman with wild, curly dark hair tried to grab it. "Damn." She gave me a shrug and moved to a smaller table at the back of the patio.

"Quick." Gage's voice rumbled near me as he set my to-go cup down.

I cleared my throat and curled my fingers around it. Better than doing something stupid like looping my finger into the worn denim about six inches from my face. Good grief.

And a flash of memory made me swallow a groan. Of me on my knees going at a very similar zipper.

Nope. Do not need that in my brain right now.

I focused on the funky to-go cup. There were about fifteen different designs on the cups, and I'd gotten almost all of them. Most of them had a small Halloween or horror item hidden in the seasonal drawings. I grinned as I spotted the skull hidden in the center of a rose.

God, I loved Macy.

"What's the smile for? I know it's not for me."

I shook my head. "Nothing."

He sat across from me, invading my space once again. Mostly because it was a little table and he had legs for freaking days. But his muscled arms and the long fingers wrapped around his cup seemed to fill every bit of the available room as well.

Everything about him was far too large. Including his ego. And other things that didn't bear repetition except in my dirtiest fantasies.

"Do you have to?"

"What?"

I glanced at his hands past the midway mark of the table.

"You liked when I invaded your space before. In fact, I nearly changed your nickname to barnacle."

"Shut up. What do you want?"

"I want you to tell me what made you smile."

"Why do you care?"

He leaned back in his chair, but his big stupid foot was still caging me into my chair. "Why wouldn't I?"

"I'm less than nothing to you. We had one night, Gage."

"Well, there's two fallacies in there. Number one, you're my sister-in-law now, so you're definitely not in the less than nothing category to me. And hello, what we did that night? Nothing forgettable there, huntress."

I flushed. "Would you stop saying stuff like that?"

"Is it that I'm mentioning it or that you can't forget it either that riles you so?"

I picked at the double shot sticker on the side of my cup. "I haven't thought of you since."

"I might believe you if you looked at me."

I lifted my gaze to his. "Not a moment since."

"Liar." He leaned forward and curled his fingers around mine. His thumb brushed over my wrist. "Because your pulse wouldn't be racing if you didn't care."

"Maybe it's stranger danger."

"I'm no stranger. Especially where my tongue has been."

"Would you keep it down?" I ducked my head and looked around.

"Oh, like you did at the wedding? I think the cat's out of the bag there."

"Yeah, well, not everyone in this café was there."

"Everyone knows."

"You underestimate your appeal to the people of this town."

He glanced around and I followed his gaze. Two women from a table over had their phones up to take a creeper picture. Another two guys were speaking in low voices as they kept sneaking glances over at us.

Not only had I slept with my future brother-in-law, but he was a celebrity to boot. There should have been all sorts of girl points to be had. And five years ago, I would have high-fived my girlfriends for bagging a hot dude with star status.

Now? I just wanted to crawl under this table.

I didn't want to be Good Time Rylee anymore. I wanted to start over and make a life somewhere. Once upon a time, I'd thought it would have been in a big city like Chicago or Portland. I wasn't really the New York City or the Los Angeles type, but a bigger city with cool places to see would be nice.

But now I really liked the idea of settling into a life where things were a little slower. Maybe even finding someone to settle down with someday. But not yet. I wanted to actually be on my own for a little while first.

Not living with my parents because I was too irresponsible to keep a job for more than three months. Or...

No. I wasn't going to think about the sleepwalking thing. I wasn't going to let that take over my life again.

"You've got a whole conversation going on in that gorgeous head of yours. Which part of it includes me?"

For once, I could give him an honest answer. "None of it."

He sat back with a half-laugh. "Good thing my ego can withstand you, huntress."

"Rylee. I know we didn't get to say names much, but let's go with Rylee." Because that nickname was far too familiar. Not to mention I didn't want to be reminded of exactly how thoroughly I'd pounced on him that night in the bar—and then at the inn.

He sipped his coffee, then gave a surprised, "Hmm."

"She's good at knowing what you need."

"I guess there's a reason why people are lined up out the door." He took another longer sip then winced.

"It's still hot, idiot."

He arched a brow at me.

I shrugged, then took a sip of my own gloriousness. Even with two shots of espresso, it wasn't bitter. I didn't know how she did it, but I spent way too much in her shop.

"What are you doing in town, Gage?"

"I told you."

"No, you gave me the answer you give to work buddies."

"I thought we weren't friends."

He had me there. I took another sip of my coffee. "True. Never mind."

He popped the top off his to-go cup and took a longer swallow.

"You're going to burn your throat."

"Will you soothe it for me? I know a few good ways."

"You're a pig."

"No, a pig would say I have a way to soothe *your* throat."

I resisted the urge to smile. I didn't want to be charmed. I'd already been charmed enough to get naked with him for a whole night. Actually, there hadn't been much need for charm. I'd been completely enamored with him from the first moment he'd bet me in a game of darts.

God, we hadn't even actually *played.* Well, I'd played with something, but it had been a bit more substantial.

And how.

I blew out a breath. "Did you really quit? From everything I've heard, you love NASCAR."

He shrugged. "Checking up on me?"

"No. Just conversations with my brother-in-law." *Lies.* I spoke to Dare approximately the same amount of words I'd shared with Gage. However, not for the same reasons. Dare just wasn't a chatty guy. My sister spoke more than enough for the both of them.

"Now I know you're lying. Dare doesn't speak."

Was he reading my mind? Luckily, I didn't have to answer. A pixie-sized woman with rainbow hair came up to our table with our food. "Hey, Ry."

"Hi, Vee."

She set a bowl with an attached basket in front of me. My perfectly crispy and gooey grilled cheese was tucked in among the bat print wax paper and a few bagel chips. My mouth watered. No wonder my pants were getting tight.

"Veronica, this is Gage. Dare's brother."

"Oh." Vee tipped her head to the side. "I don't see the resemblance."

She wasn't wrong. Dare was a little stockier than Gage. My lunch date—*companion*—was long and lean with dark eyes and dark blond hair that would probably be curly if he let it grow out.

And I was looking at him far too closely.

Gage popped one of the bagel chips in his mouth with a grin. "And Dare is glad every damn day."

"Well, nice to meet ya. Enjoy the food. Give a holler if you need anything." She gave him a little wave and did the look beneath her lashes thing and I wanted to toss a chip at her head.

"Thanks." Oddly, his gaze didn't move from me. And I wasn't sure how I felt about that.

I looked away from his way too intense stare and dunked a bagel chip into my tomato bisque. "Stop looking at me like that."

"Like what?"

"Like there's some joke and I'm not in on it."

"Only joke is you checked up on me and don't want to own up to it."

"Are we still talking about that?" I gave him a bored look.

He picked up his sandwich with a half grin. "No. I don't need any more details. Just knowing is enough."

"You're an ass."

"I've been called worse." He made a low hum and dunked his grilled cheese in the soup.

"I swear I've gained ten pounds just living over this place."

His eyebrows shot up. "So, you moved here too? Not just work?"

"Yep. I've got my own place in the apartments above." And I was proud of it. It was a small place, barely big enough for me and all my junk. But it was mine, and I paid for it out of my savings and pittance of a paycheck.

Thankfully, I had quite a bit in savings. Living at home for most of my life had some perks. My parents were more worried about me having a savings account than making me pay rent to them.

"I wouldn't mind seeing it."

"I bet you wouldn't. We aren't going there, Gage."

"You're the one with the dirty mind."

"Right."

"What's the harm? I mean, we know we're good together."

"We're not just two strangers anymore. We're family. And God, that's gross, but you know what I mean. We have to see each other for Christmas and Thanksgiving and every other holiday that includes food."

"What's that got to do with us revisiting our very hot, very compatible relationship?"

I took an exorbitantly long time to chew my next bite. Because he wasn't wrong. We *were* blazing hot together during that one night. But that was all it was, one night. It wasn't anything to base a relationship on. Or a repeat performance.

"That busy brain is working overtime again, Ry. I remember you being much more impulsive."

"Yes, well, that was when I didn't know who you were." And also, when I happened to be a little inebriated.

"So, the driver thing is a problem?"

"No." I put my corner of crusty goodness down. "Besides, you're not a driver anymore you just said."

"Right. So, the unemployed thing is a problem?"

"Do not be obtuse. You know it's because of our siblings being… oh, I don't know, married. We are a crash and burn and you know it. You probably haven't had a girlfriend that lasted more than a weekend since you started your career. And based on some of the articles I've read, I have some proof of it."

"First of all, you really did read up on me. Secondly, those click-bait articles are just that. Bait. I haven't been with half of the women they say I've been with."

"And yet there's still half of that number and it's a big freaking number."

"You didn't know jack about me when we met, and it didn't matter."

"It didn't matter because it was one and done, remember?"

"So, we'll go for a fifth round. I believe it was four that night."

"I'm not interested in going for another round."

"You wouldn't be this heated up about it if you weren't."

I snapped my jaw shut. He had a point. And okay, so a teeny part of me would love to drag him upstairs and find out if he could still do that thing with his fingers and tongue at the same time. But that teeny part wasn't worth the fallout.

Because a guy like Gage was exactly who Good Time Rylee would get wound up about. He was fine to have fun with, but once the fun was over, he would be gone. So far gone.

"You're just bored." I stood up with my cup. "And I'm not going to be the girl you waste time with while you figure out what you want."

He sat up straighter. "Rylee, wait—"

I shoved my chair in. "My break is over. Thanks for lunch." I weaved my way through the tables to the edge of the half wall that blocked off the café from the sidewalk.

He didn't follow me, just as I'd known he wouldn't.

Because guys like him were all the same.

FIVE

I PICKED AT MY SANDWICH FOR A FEW MORE MINUTES. WHAT HAD ONCE tasted like buttery perfection now was more like sawdust.

I kicked at the chair across from me.

"You're a dipshit."

I looked up and groaned. "How much of that did you hear?"

"Enough." Dare pulled out the chair Rylee had been sitting on and twirled it around so he could straddle it. "But that's only one of your bonehead moves this week. Or this month."

I tipped my head back. "So, I guess you heard."

Dare looked down at the bowl in front of him. "Did she even eat any of this?"

"Nope."

Dare shrugged and picked up the spoon. "Shame to waste it."

I rolled my eyes. "Who told you?"

Dare popped a bagel chip into his mouth before tucking into the soup. "Mom."

"I told her not to say anything."

Dare gave me a look. "Uh-huh."

I picked up my sandwich again. At least it would fill the hole in my gut. I'd driven straight up from the city. "I was trying to surprise her with a visit."

"Oh, you'll do that, all right."

"I'm not stupid, Dare."

He just grunted.

"I have offers for other teams."

"Obviously, they're just offers if you're up here instead of figuring out a new car."

"I deserve some time off."

"Don't pout. I didn't say shit."

He didn't have to.

Besides, I'd said all of it to myself as I was driving cross-country. Only one of the reasons I couldn't stand my own company anymore.

We ate in silence for a few minutes.

"Don't mess with Ry."

I set my spoon down. "Are you warning me off her?"

"Yep."

"Little late for that."

Dare looked up from his bowl. "Exactly. She doesn't need your pile of crap right now. She's got enough to deal with."

"What's that supposed to mean? And what's her crap?"

"She just moved here last week. She's staying in Kel's old place. Took over the lease."

"So, she moved in. Perfect time for—"

"For you?" He shook his head with a laugh. "She's a good kid. It's bad enough you two made a spectacle at my wedding. We don't need that kind of drama at Christmas dinners. Get me?"

"Jeez, is there some handbook for Christmas I didn't get?"

"You haven't been around since you were seventeen. You don't exactly get the family dynamic thing."

"Who the hell are you? Family dynamic? What the hell does that mean?"

Since when did my brother grow a vocabulary? This had to be the most words I'd ever heard out of his mouth that didn't include car parts.

Dare sighed. "Don't get me wrong. I'm all for a visit, but she's Kel's sister. Her *only* sister. She's not one of your race girls who is aware of the score."

She'd been damn well aware of the score when she asked me to be her one-night stand. Because it hadn't been me asking. I didn't say no, but I hadn't been the instigator.

"I—"

Dare held up his hand. "I don't want to know the hows and whys. It's over, let it stay over, huh?" He tugged off the top of his to-go cup and took a long drink. "Visit with mom. Hell, you could do a few things around the old house to help out if you're bored. But stay out of Rylee's..."

"Pants?"

Dare gave me a hard stare. "Life."

"She's a big girl. She can tell me to go fuck myself."

He folded his hands around the cup. "I believe she did that a few minutes before I sat down, brother."

I resisted the urge to snarl at him. Because she had told me to take a hike, but more because I'd assumed we could just continue our good time. Getting shot down was a rarity for me, but it had happened a time or two.

I could usually let it roll off of me. There was always someone who was interested whether I was into them or not.

My whole fucking life had been easy, to be honest. Once Dare had stepped out of the light, I'd smoothly sailed right into the driver position for Patton, Inc. And I'd happily been their golden boy for two years before I moved on to another company—and finally been lured away by an even bigger corporation.

It didn't matter who they were. All I cared about was the cars. At least that was all I used to care about. I wasn't even sure when it stopped being about driving. It just felt like an endless merry-go-round of races and practice. Even the amount of down time seemed to get shorter every year. Special races kept popping up for chances at bigger winnings.

And I'd chased them all until the wins didn't mean a damn thing.

I sounded like an asshole even to myself but winning truly didn't mean anything anymore. Just another day at the office. And that was why I knew I had to walk away.

When driving one of the most impressive machines on the goddamn planet was like riding a desk? Nope.

Time to go.

"I'm not looking to cause trouble. I just haven't been around my family for a while."

"Whose fault is that?"

I sighed. "I know. Not like you and Wes came to one of my races."

Dare looked down at his coffee cup. "Yeah, well, raising a kid and owning a house doesn't leave much room for fun in the bank."

"I would have—"

"Don't."

Yeah, my prideful brother wouldn't let me spend my money on him. Not like I should be surprised there. "Well, I'm here now. I'll even watch Wes if you and Kel want a date night before she pops. She's due soon, isn't she?"

"A few more months."

"Yeah, so you guys need some couple-time."

"I don't know."

"Wes's what? Seven now?" Christ, how could he be seven already?

"At least you can count."

"Helps when I'm doing laps."

"So, what are you going to do now, genius? Counting laps is quite the résumé."

"Very funny. Neither one of us were just drivers."

Dare snapped his top back on his coffee. "No, we were not. But that wasn't an answer either."

"I'll figure it out."

"Mmm." He stood and swung the chair around. "Go see Ma."

"Already on the schedule. Even got her some flowers."

"Suck up."

I waggled my eyebrows. "I'm the favorite kid for a reason, man."

"You keep telling yourself that." He gave me a two-finger salute and headed out of the café.

Well, that wasn't the reunion I'd been looking for with my brother. Then again, things between us hadn't been amazing since he'd gotten off the circuit. Nothing overly stress-inducing. We just didn't have a lot in common anymore. Once he'd been out of racing, he'd been completely out.

I wasn't sure he even still watched the races. In fact, I'd bet my Daytona trophy he didn't.

Because I wasn't an asshole, I took our dishes inside and stopped to get another one of Macy's magic potions. The worst of the lunch rush had cleared out and the tiny rainbow-haired girl was refilling the bakery case.

She popped up when she saw me. "Hey. Oh, thanks, you can put them in that bucket on the end."

"Sure." I moved back to the front of the counter. "I'm not sure what your boss—at least I'm pretty sure she was the boss…"

"Dark hair. Looks like she sucks on a lemon thirty hours a day?"

I pressed my lips together against a laugh. "Now that you mention it."

"Macy. Don't worry. I say it to her face all the time."

Macy herself appeared from the back room. "She does. She's unaware of how to behave in a professional manner."

I laughed. "I was wondering if you could make me another one of these." I held up my cup. "Not sure what it is, but it's glorious."

"Sure."

"And another of whatever you made for Rylee."

She looked over her shoulder. "Sure about that, ace?"

"Maybe lighten up on the espresso part." And while I was fairly sure she'd control herself, based on past experience with her there was a small chance she could aim for my head. No need to give her any more stimulants.

Unless it was of an organic nature.

"Your funeral."

"Did you see our little fight too?"

She came back with two more to-go cups. "You're new to Crescent Cove. And while I've only been here a few months, I can tell you one thing I've learned." She set the cups in front of me. "Nothing stays a secret."

I swapped two cups for a twenty. "I'm getting that."

"Don't piss off my friend. I have fake IDs and four different forms of solvent in my back room."

I almost laughed, then it lodged in my throat. Not sure Macy was the joking kind. "Yes, ma'am."

"Have a nice day." Her smile was a little scary. Like she didn't do it much.

I took the cups and forced myself not to look back. Only the weak looked back at a predator.

I headed toward my car. I'd have walked it, but I had a feeling the lovely Kathy was taking me at my word with a huge floral arrangement. Good thing my credit card was ready for it.

I found a spot on the street near the floral shop, parked, grabbed our coffees and backed my way into the shop. Rylee was back at her station, her jaw set and her ear pods in to block out the world.

I wasn't sure I wanted to press my luck any more today. Perhaps taking a little advice was prudent. I set her coffee next to her and headed for the large arrangement. Pretty sure that one was mine.

"Mr. Kramer!"

"Gage, please."

Kathy clasped her hands in front of her chest. "Gage. I hope Melissa loves the arrangement. I added a few flowers I know she loves."

"Just a few, huh?"

She shrugged with a little giggle. "Yes, well, it's not every day that her famous son comes home to visit."

I glanced over at Rylee, but she resolutely worked her baskets and wouldn't look at me. I was pretty sure she'd moved that same flower to five different spots, so she knew I was there.

I pulled out my wallet and handed over my credit card. "I'm sure my mother will love it."

"I'm so pleased." Kathy rushed around to the register and cashed me out. I resisted the urge to make Rylee talk to me. The urge to tease a smile out of her was a little too strong, but I tamped it down.

I did catch her looking when I backed my way out the door, arrangement in hand. She didn't even attempt to help me. Even when Kathy bustled forward, admonishing her, Rylee barely batted an eye.

Damn, I liked her. A masochist, that was me.

I checked in at my folks' pizza joint, but my mom wasn't working tonight. Perfect. I'd actually be able to surprise her.

The drive to Laurel was familiar and soothing. I enjoyed my coffee, though I still didn't know what was in it. Perhaps I should worry now that I knew of Macy's murderous tendencies, but whatever was going on with the dark roast, I didn't much care. It was the best coffee I'd ever had.

The country roads were wet and clear. The snow had melted away with the endless rain that had been sitting over New York since I'd been back. The days were getting longer as spring muscled its way into the Northeast.

Some of the houses weren't quite as rundown here in Laurel as I remembered. New tenants or people aging out, I wasn't sure. Either way, it seemed as if my old hometown was making a bit of a comeback. Or maybe it was just fresh eyes.

I'd run far and fast from here, that was for sure.

I pulled up the gravel drive. The familiar bark of Sandy, my parents' golden retriever, made me smile as I pushed open the door.

"Hiya, girl." She jumped and spun in circles then gave me a hard lean as she licked my face off.

"Gage? Is that you?"

"Nothing like ruining the surprise," I muttered to the dog. I smiled as my mom came down the stairs of the porch. "Hey, Ma."

"What are you doing here?" She rushed across the uneven pavers to catch me in a fierce, hard hug. Nothing quite like a mom hug when you didn't know what the hell was up with the universe.

I lowered my forehead to her shoulder for a second and dragged in her familiar scent. Dove soap and Estee Lauder. I knew, because I sent her a bottle every year for her birthday.

I squeezed her back and spun her around. Her girlish laugh lifted the rock that I hadn't realized was sitting on my chest. "How are you, beautiful?"

"I'm happy to have my youngest home." She stepped away from me enough that she could frame my head in her hands. "That wanderlust is still in your eyes."

"If that wanderlust means sitting on that huge, perfect recliner in the living room, then you would be correct."

"You know it's not." She frowned. "Well, come on. I just made some banana bread."

"With chocolate chips?"

"Is there any other kind?"

"Not as far as I'm concerned." I gave her a smacking kiss on the cheek. "One second. I have something for you."

"You don't have to bring me presents every time you come home. This time, it's not Christmas, Lucas Gage Kramer."

I winced. "I don't think this rates my full name." I ducked into the backseat where I'd buckled in her huge basket. I stepped back and closed the door. Her gasp and quick rush of tears told me I had chosen right.

Or Kathy had.

"All right, no tears, woman."

"They're beautiful. And so big."

"Yeah, well, a woman named Kathy had my number."

"I just bet that woman did."

I kissed my mom's temple and urged her forward. "Some things never change."

"Does your father know you're here?"

"Nope. Had to surprise my best girl first."

My mom gave me a narrow-eyed glance. "Hmm."

"What?"

"When your charm gets gooey, my mom antennae goes buzzy."

"Then it should always buzz."

"It does when it comes to you."

I laughed, then it turned into a groan at the scent of fresh banana bread. "Man, it's good to be home."

"I really am glad you're home, sweetie."

I set the flowers down on the large shelf under the picture window in the living room. "Me too, Mom."

I really hadn't been aware just how much I needed home until just this second.

And maybe not entirely because of my family and familiar comforts. Perhaps being home would bring some new into my life as well.

Or it already had.

SIX

I LOVED THE IDEA OF LIVING ALONE. THE ACTUALITY OF IT SOMETIMES was a bit more than I was prepared for. Especially since my window faced Main Street. Small town life didn't exactly mean a lot of nightlife or traffic, but oddly, it was the water that freaked me out the most.

I could hear it all the time.

Boats bumping against the dock and water forever swishing. People usually liked that lapping noise. For God's sake, there were a million sleeping apps that actually accentuated any and all water sounds.

I knew that, because I had all the fucking apps.

Because I didn't know how to sleep. Insomnia had always been a problem for me. Whenever I did manage to doze off, the water kept sneaking into my dreams. And dreams were forever a worry now.

So, I'd set a trap for myself. Much as I used to as a kid.

Unfortunately, I was too smart in my dreams. I wished the wakeful Rylee was half as brainy.

I curled into the large papasan chair I'd set up in front of the window and tried to chill myself out. Sometimes when there simply wasn't a place to go, my subconscious would let me sleep. I pulled the light blanket up around me and slipped in my air pods.

Rain app on the go, full moon in the sky over the lake. I just needed a few hours down and I could make it through the day. I resisted the urge to look at the time on my phone. It made sleeping even more difficult.

Don't fight it.

My eyes got heavier, and the moon blurred in the sky.

"I don't have time for your bullshit, Gage. I told you what you needed to do for Ma."

"And I've been working on the house for the last three days. I'm a fucking driver and mechanic, not a handyman, asshole."

"Then go fucking *be* a driver. It's what you do, right?"

I opened one eye. Gage?

I sat up as the voices lowered and faded. Had I been dreaming of him? Not shocking. I'd had some crazy hot dreams the first few weeks after our hookup.

Well, I was still in the chair. That was one good thing. The sun was streaming into my apartment. I must have slept. And hey, I hadn't gotten up in the middle of the night.

I hoped.

I climbed out of the chair and looked around for any of the telltale signs. I had a habit of doing weird decorating things. And then I saw my fridge was open. It certainly hadn't been when I went to bed.

Dammit.

"Great." I cringed at all the food I'd probably have to throw out.

I stepped around the temple of plastic cups near my door and quickly stacked them to put on my kitchen island for later. Luckily, I'd taken a shower the night before, so I just had to brush my teeth and get dressed.

My hair was heinous, but that was what messy buns were for.

I grabbed my bag and hurried down the stairs and out the front door, checking my phone. There were two messages from Kathy already. Shit.

"You come into town, thinking you can just have a good time. Some of us have more to worry about."

My eyebrows shot up. I wasn't sure I'd ever heard Dare raise his voice. So, it hadn't been a dream after all. And they were *still* arguing.

"Who said anything about a good time? I've had sheetrock dust on my clothes for days, fuckhead." Gage's usually smooth, flirty voice was harsh and stressed.

Yeah, I didn't want anything to do with sibling fights. I'd had plenty with my sister.

Besides, I needed to save my energy to deal with Kathy.

I tried to sneak past but caught Dare's attention. His face went from snarly to a cool, chilled mask.

"Don't mind me, guys."

Gage turned around. "Rylee." His eyes still fired with temper, but exhaustion lined them. Maybe he wasn't getting any sleep either. And a beard was quickly forming out of his perpetual scruff.

"I should probably thank you. Your little argument was quite the alarm clock." I tapped my wrist. "I've got to get going."

Dare's ears went pink. "I don't have time for this shit." He turned on his heel and headed back to the garage.

Gage sighed and turned back to me. "Can I walk you to work?"

"No, I'm good." I secured my purse on my shoulder and the sidewalk suddenly shifted under me. I tried to catch myself on the back panel of the silver car parked on the street, but a swarm of black dots and Gage's sharp, "Jesus," were the last things I was aware of.

Next thing I knew, my cheek was pressed into a very warm neck and I was definitely not on my feet.

"I've got you."

I pressed my lips against the whiskers hidden in the soft material of a collared shirt. The sweet scent of cherries dented the fog, followed by the sharp tang of his cologne.

I knew that scent.

I'd practically climbed inside of it that one night. I couldn't get enough of him. "Gage?"

"That's right. You all right?" He shifted me closer. His strong arms strained under my weight.

Oh, God. Too many mocha lattes. The guy was gonna tumble under me like a redwood. "What happened?"

"I think you fainted."

"I did not."

"Okay, you just gracefully folded into a human accordion on the street." He shifted me again. "Is there some sort of way to get into your building? Key or something?"

"I've got to go to work."

"Yeah, well, it's either up into your place or I bring you into the café."

"Upstairs."

"What I thought."

"Where's my bag?"

He lifted his shoulder. "Got it."

I wanted to crawl right into the cracks in the sidewalk. "I'm okay. You can put me down now."

"Nope. We're going to get you upstairs and get some sugar into you. You're not doing one of those stupid juice cleanses or air diets, right?"

"What? You think I need a diet?" What the heck was an air diet anyway?

"God, no. You're fucking beautiful."

Slightly mollified, I huffed out a growl. "Then what the hell?"

"Because you fainted on the sidewalk, Ry. You probably didn't eat."

Well, he had me there. I hadn't eaten, but I didn't even have a headache. I couldn't be that hungry. And based on the condition of my fridge this morning, I'd definitely eaten something last night. How the hell was I supposed to explain that?

Oh, don't worry, I'm like a zombie past midnight except I stress-eat PBJs instead of brains. No big.

Rather than address the peanut butter-flavored elephant sitting in my belly, I nodded at my bag still over his shoulder. "My keys have a security fob."

He backed into the panel and lifted his shoulder to get the keys near the sensor. When the door opened, he maneuvered us inside and up the stairs as if I didn't weigh a damn thing. His muscles rippled under my thighs and his grip was nice and secure.

I'd never felt so safe in my life.

He needed to put me down now. These definitely were not the feelings I wanted to have for this man.

"Look, I just didn't sleep great last night."

"Why? Thinking about me?"

"You wish."

"I do." His gaze dropped to my mouth then back to my eyes. "Especially if they're dirty thoughts." He grinned. "Door locked?"

"No."

He sighed. "Not exactly smart."

"Small town."

"Still weirdos in small towns. Don't you watch television?"

"Wait, you mean like weirdos who insist on carrying women around and then ply them with sugar behind closed doors? Guys like that?" I smiled. "Nope, never heard of that sort."

"Smart ass." He juggled me enough to get his hand around the doorknob.

"I could stand up." But he was already on his way inside.

Sack of potatoes for the win.

He kicked the door shut behind us and crossed my apartment in two strides, setting me on the couch. He cupped my face and tipped my chin up so he could look me right in the eyes. "There you are. You don't resemble a piece of paper anymore. I like the golden color you usually have."

When he stared at me just a little too long, then his gaze dropped to my mouth again, I batted his hands away. "I'm fine."

Instead of going in for the kiss I knew he wanted—nope. Not going there again. I would not be swayed.

Probably.

I was almost sure.

He rested his lips against my forehead. "No fever."

"I have a mom, thanks."

He gave me a long, level stare. "You do not have maternal or paternal thoughts around me, huntress."

I shivered, which only made him grin wider.

He set my purse on the floor. "I'll get you something to drink."

"Not the milk," I called after him. That definitely needed to go down the sink. Of course I'd just bought it.

"Got it." He came back with a soda. "It's not very cold."

"I just put it in there."

"You were running late you said."

I took the can but ignored his comment. "Thanks for the assist. I'm not sure what happened."

He sat next to me, making the couch feel even smaller than usual. Why was he so…big?

Yeah, no need for those sorts of thoughts. First, you started off innocently pondering toned muscles. Then, oh, maybe his hands. Large hands capable of framing your face while you kissed or holding your thighs open, depending where the kiss occurred.

Next thing you knew, you were dwelling on penis size. It was a slope guaranteed to make me slippery.

No, thanks.

"Nice place."

I opened the can and took a sip of the sweet soda. I'd never had trouble with blood sugar before. I drank until the lingering shakes faded and my brain felt clearer.

"I feel better. I need to get to work."

"Work? You almost passed out in the middle of the fucking street."

My cheeks burned. "Thanks for reminding me."

He stood and paced the very cramped space between my couch and kitchen island. "Jesus, Ry. I think your boss would understand."

I dug into my purse for my phone. A third call was coming in. "Hi, Kathy."

"Where are you?"

I winced. "Something came up."

"*Something?* That's unacceptable, Rylee."

"I know, I'm sorry. I..." I didn't want to tell her I overslept then fainted. It didn't sound good.

Gage plucked the phone out of my hand. "Hi, Kathy, is it?"

I stood up and wobbled a little. "Dammit, give me that."

Gage turned away from me. "I'll bring Rylee down to the shop in a few minutes. She's just had a little accident." He went silent for a minute then said a few *mmm-hmms.* "I knew you'd understand. She'll be in as soon as she can. Thanks, you too." He handed me back the phone. "Have you never called in before?"

I grabbed it and this time, my feet stayed under me even after the quick move. "How dare you?"

"Me? I just got you out of trouble."

"Oh, sure. You just lied to her. I didn't have an accident."

"Technically, you did. I saved you."

"You—I..." Stunned, I stalked over to him. "Get out."

"Ah, there's your color back."

I had to be red, because I was so mad, I was going to rip his eyeballs out.

He curled his arm around my waist. "You scared the crap out of me, Ry."

I wanted to push him back, but the honest worry on his face stopped me. "It was no big deal. I just haven't been sleeping well like I told you."

He grazed his fingers along my cheek to tip my head up. His ridiculously long fingers slipped into the wispy hair falling from my topknot. "Why?"

"I never sleep well."

"Well, I've only spent one night with you and we definitely didn't sleep."

I wrapped my fingers around his wrist. "Gage—"

"Well, we didn't."

"I thought we weren't discussing that."

"No, I think that was your idea. Me? I want to talk about it all day long. All night long. Hell, any hour you want."

I couldn't stop the laugh. "Stop trying to be charming."

"I don't try. It's just a God given talent."

I rolled my eyes, but then he was lowering his mouth. Before I could push him away or evade, his lips touched mine. Not the hot, hard kisses that we'd shared before.

No, this was soft and sweet.

A barely there kiss, but the memories it stirred made me lightheaded again. I swayed against him and he tugged me closer.

"You're not going to faint on me again," he said against my mouth.

"And you ruined it." I pushed him back.

His laugh was low and rumbly. "So, I just made you swoon then?"

"Go."

He tugged on my knot and my hair tumbled over my shoulders. "Jesus, you are stunning."

I wasn't sure what to say to that. I nibbled on my lower lip and resisted the urge to bring my fingers to my still buzzing mouth.

"I'll check on you later." He gave me that half smile that had gotten me into so much trouble to begin with, then he was gone.

I collapsed back on the sofa with a groan. "What are you doing, Rylee?"

SEVEN

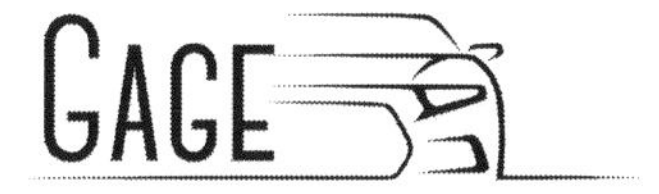

FOR A MINUTE, I WAITED IN THE HALL.

Like that parental figure she accused me of being? Or like a boyfriend?

Nah. Like a...friend.

Much better.

I really didn't want to leave her alone. Watching her crumple like that had taken ten years off me, man. I was used to her railing at me, not going as pale as Casper and sagging as if her bones had dissolved.

I pressed my forehead to her door and inhaled and exhaled until my still-racing heart leveled out. Then I made myself go downstairs.

Rylee was indestructible. A ballbuster with a mouth to match. It had taken everything inside me to get up and walk out after touching her. And not because I wanted to peel her out of those tight jeans and the sweater falling off her shoulder.

Okay, so I always wanted to peel her out of her clothes.

But I also wanted to tuck her in bed and make her sleep away the circles under her eyes. And I wasn't that guy. Sleepovers meant clinging and expectations and I was never around long enough for that.

But things were changing in my life.

And if my stupid, stubborn brother would give me a chance to help him, I might just find a reason to stick around. I really wished she hadn't heard us fighting this morning, but then again, if she hadn't, I wouldn't have had a chance to be there for her.

My gut dropped into my toes and I had to steady myself on the front door of her building. What if I hadn't been there and she'd fallen into the street?

I couldn't think about that. I *had* been there, and it didn't seem as if it was a usual occurrence for her to rely on someone else—even for a few minutes.

Sleep deprivation could mess you up. I knew that all too well. Not because I normally had trouble sleeping, but when I was deep in figuring out a problem with my car, I'd spent a string of nights working it out with the engineer on my team. I had a knack with motors, but with new high-tech electronics making everything more complex, well...there were some things above my capabilities. Then getting behind the wheel—yeah, I'd pulled some bonehead moves in my time.

Rylee seemed more practical than that, so I assumed she hadn't been intentionally burning the candle at both ends. I could only hope she had a touch of some flu. I'd know soon enough since I couldn't keep my lips off of her.

"Fucking animal," I muttered as I pushed open the door.

Instead of heading out to my car, I went into J&T's Auto. I wasn't done talking to my brother. He was surly as shit, but even more so than usual. I hadn't been around much, and he'd shouldered a lot of the responsibilities in our family. Our parents were getting older, but they definitely weren't ready for the old folks' home.

My mother probably would run whichever one she ended up in anyway.

Besides, I'd been at their house for the last few days. The Honey-Do list was extensive enough for me to know Dare had been dealing with his own stuff. Maybe it was just nerves due to another kid on the way, but it felt like something else.

Dare under stress grunted more and put his head down to do the work. Today, his eyes had been a little wild and panicked. And I wasn't used to seeing that when it came to my big brother.

Time to find out the score.

The change from bright spring daylight to the dank garage made me squint. Instead of my brother, I found the heavyset owner, his shock of white hair nearly standing straight up, flicking through an order book.

"Hey, old man. Where's my brother?"

"Well, if it isn't the fancy pants race car driver. Decided to hang up your helmet?"

I shrugged. "At least for now."

"If you're looking for a place for cars, come talk to me."

I frowned. "Why?"

"Didn't Dare tell you?"

Ding-ding. I knew something was up. "You selling?"

"Yeah, time for this old man to retire. All these cars are just computers these days. And no one wants to pay a decent mechanic. Get their tune-ups at the car wash combo oil change places these days."

"Good to know. Not sure what I'd do with a garage."

"You don't have a bunch of fancy cars?"

I laughed. "No, I didn't waste my money on a fleet of cars like some of the drivers."

He scratched the back of his head, so his hair stood up even more. "Huh. Well, that's a surprise."

"I don't like to be predictable."

"Evidently not." He nodded toward the back of the shop. "Your brother's in the back junkyard looking for some lug nut he swears is out there."

I followed the sound of banging. My brother had climbed up on a rusted-out shell of a car. He was kicking a crowbar the size of my damn leg.

"What the hell are you doing?"

"It's rusted..." He grunted as he tried for more leverage. "On."

The squeak of metal grinding killed me. "Jesus. Let me help."

“I don’t need your help.”

“Oscar.”

“What did you call me?”

“Oscar, you know—”

“I know.” He frowned and ripped open his work shirt and tossed it over the hood of the next car over.

“Big man can do his work now that those pesky sleeves aren’t in the way.”

“Fuck off.” But Dare’s mouth twitched a little.

Bastard just wouldn’t lighten up about anything.

I let him get some of his frustrations out on the rusty lug nut and picked up his shirt off the hood of the old Ford. “What the hell are you guys doing with a ’41 Ford back here?”

“Fucking fuck.” Dare wiped his forehead with the back of his forearm and jumped down. “What are you crying about?”

“Get it off?”

He gave me a bored look and rattled the lug nuts in his hand.

“Look at you. Didn’t even bleed.”

“If I wanted this kind of abuse, I’d be home with my kid.” He peered over my shoulder. “That rust bucket?”

“Dude, it’s a hot rod.”

“It *was* a hot rod.” Dare grabbed back his shirt. “Now it’s a rusty nightmare.”

“Do you have any idea how much people pay for these things? Even just for parts, it’s worth a couple grand.”

He shrugged. “I’ll let Jerome know. Maybe he can put out some feelers before…” He fell silent.

“I heard.”

Dare speared his hands into his pockets. “Yeah. Fucking timing. I didn’t think he’d be retiring for a few more years.”

“So, buy it.”

“What? No.” He blew out a breath. “I put my name out to a few places, but garages aren’t what they used to be, man.”

“If you actually used your contacts, you’d have more business than you could handle.”

"Yeah, well, I have a family. I can't be working fourteen hours a day on stock cars. And those grease monkeys never have money. They always want to trade favors. I am not about that life."

"You're wasted here."

"Don't start."

"Jesus, Dare. You've still got the best hands in the business. You know how to pull apart an engine and rebuild it like fucking *MacGyver*."

"I like working nine to five and going the hell home."

"I don't believe you."

"I don't care what you believe. Don't start blowing smoke here when you know you'll be gone in a few weeks."

"How do you know that? You don't know shit about me."

How could he, when I was still figuring out my next steps myself?

"Whose fault is that? And people don't change."

"Obviously, they do. The Dare I remember was excited about being under the hood of a car. Now you do oil changes like Valvoline."

Dare twisted my shirt and pushed me back against the hot rod. "I take care of my family. I stick. Unlike you."

I shoved him back, my heart racing. I hadn't come back here to get into a fight with my brother, dammit. "Don't."

He backed up, his jaw tight. "Don't talk shit about stuff you know nothing about. You've been the golden boy on the racing circuit for years. You don't know what it's like to work and worry. So, don't give me some crap advice about me being a good mechanic."

I opened my mouth, but Dare sliced his hand through the air. "Enough. Get the fuck out of here."

But I didn't have a chance, because Dare stalked out first.

I slammed my hand on the rusted hood of the car. Well, that went well. I knew better than to push at my brother. He needed to think it was his idea. But I knew he was wasting his talents here. I hadn't been blowing smoke about that.

With one last sigh, I smoothed my hand down the scoop of the hood. Rat rods were in big demand. Between the two of us, we could trick it out and sell it for ten or twenty times what we'd pay for the parts.

The garage and the junkyard were perfect for working on them.

I scrubbed my hands over my hair. Lately, I was striking out everywhere when it came to people. But for the first time in a long damn time, I was excited.

This was something I knew how to do.

And I knew plenty of guys who had money to burn on stupid cars that were tricked out and one of a kind. Even better, I knew of a handful of people who might be interested in working on the cars. Custom fabrication was fucking expensive, but I had the start-up money. Especially when I had the perfect person to do it up right.

I pulled out my phone and dug through my contacts. This kind of thing required more than a text.

On the third ring, a purring voice came on the line. "Has hell frozen over?"

"Hey, Burns. How're things?"

"Boring."

"You're no good at being bored."

Her throaty laugh boomed in my ear. "No, I am not. Got some trouble in mind?"

"Maybe. How fast can you get to upstate New York?"

"New York? Crap. I don't know, couple days."

"Well, get on that big beautiful bike of yours and come see me. I'll text you the address."

"You better make it worth my time."

"Don't I always?"

"No."

"Burns…"

"Okay, yes. But I still think we would be better naked friends."

"You'd chew me up and spit me out. Pass."

Her throaty laugh was her reply. She hung up on me. I grinned as I shoved my phone into my pocket and headed up the sidewalk to Brewed Awakening.

Tish Burns was as scary as she was beautiful, but she was also one of my oldest friends. I wouldn't fuck that up by sleeping with her.

Besides, the only one I wanted to get naked with lately was a crazy dark-haired siren. It was time to check up on her with a little coffee in hand.

Surely my luck had to be in somewhere today.

EIGHT

"These need to be done by three." Kathy dumped two baskets and a three-foot vase on my worktable.

"Three?"

"If you were here on time, it wouldn't have been an issue. Monty already has a funeral order and I'm working on the Jenkins wedding for tomorrow."

I bit down on my tongue. "Got it."

I'd been over three hours late. Kathy didn't care about my excuses. To be honest, I couldn't blame her. I'd been pushing the no sleep thing for too many days. Too afraid to doze off for long in case I tried to sneak into Macy's place again. Now I was even more afraid of trying to break in. She'd had to change the codes and add the cameras to cover her own ass.

Me wandering around was just plain dangerous, especially with stairs in the mix. I'd jerry-rigged an alarm on my front door. So far, I hadn't gone down the steps again, but I'd been hitting the fridge pretty hard. My famous peanut butter knives were back in the drawer. I'd even found a potted plant in my crisper before I left for work.

The more I freaked about it, the more it spiraled, but I couldn't calm down and sleep.

I pulled my phone out and opened up the meditation podcast I'd found. Maybe if I found my center, I could find my pillow without putting it in the fridge too.

I grabbed my pail and headed for the cooler. Eh, this wouldn't do right now. The meditation podcast made me want to crawl up on one of the carts and take a nap, so I switched it out for my favorite true crime podcast. Separating out the flowers I needed according to the form was monotonous and soothing, and the case details gave my busy brain a focus.

By the time I hefted the overflowing pail and returned to my workstation, I was invested in the missing person's case and ready to make these arrangements my bitch. I didn't mind the bigger projects. It gave me time to stretch my design capabilities. My grandmother had been a florist and taught me the difference between a mum and a carnation before I could read. Following her around the shop and our conversations as we fussed with flowers were some of my favorite memories.

I still wasn't sure what I wanted to be when I grew up, but this would do for now.

I'd been in every level of retail hell from food service to department stores. I'd done the call center thing, tried insurance temp agencies, and doctor's offices. I'd even sold ad space at a radio station for six months before the host of the channel had hit on me one too many times. I'd left the mic open during one of his more salacious come-ons and gotten his ass fired.

After that, I'd received a polite severance package with more zeroes than my time there merited to go on my way without suing. I took it as hazard pay and padded my nest egg.

I'd squirreled away information from all of them, but nothing ever quite clicked. Flowers came the closest.

And now I had to prove myself yet again. Seemed that was what I was always doing to get out of one scrape or another.

"What are you doing?"

I pulled my earbud out of my ear. "The main arrangement."

"You're using too many lilies. This is a three-hundred-dollar piece, not five-hundred. Trim that down and fill with the alstroemerias."

"But those look chintzy with the callas."

"Not if you do it right. And they're far more affordable. If you fill in with other flowers, they look just as pretty."

I snapped my jaw shut and tugged out the blooms. I'd done a damn good job and it was well within the budget she'd listed. Fucking cheap ass.

"I can hear what you're thinking. You're already on thin ice, young lady."

Oh, she couldn't hear what I was thinking. And that was a good thing.

Kathy swiped the lilies off my table and marched to the back to put them back in the cooler.

The bell over the door jangled and I shut my eyes. "What are you doing here?"

Gage came in with a pair of to-go cups. "Bribing my favorite girl."

"I'm not your girl." But I took the cup greedily. I was so blasted tired. I could literally curl up under my table and take a nap. Maybe I could sleepwalk my way through the shitty floral arrangement I had to do.

Then again, I'd probably use up all the lilies. My sleeping self was smart enough to avoid boobytraps, I bet she had exquisite taste too.

"How are you feeling?"

"I'm fine. You don't have to worry about me."

"Tell that to the three of my nine lives you murdered when you—"

I slapped my hand over his mouth. "Can you not?"

He nipped at my fingers. "I remember the last time you put your hand over my mouth. Oh, wait, it was me putting my hand over *your* mouth because you were screaming loud enough to bring security."

I stomped on his foot and peered around the corner for Kathy. "Are you trying to get me into trouble?"

He grinned and lifted my wrist to his lips. He flicked his tongue over my pulse point before letting my hand free as Kathy came out, whistling.

I fisted my hand and moved back to my workstation.

"Oh, Mr. Kramer. What are you doing back?"

"Harassing my favorite florist." He lifted his cup of coffee. "Just bringing her a pick-me-up."

"Is this why you were late, Rylee?"

Because I'd slept through three alarms? Yeah, that probably wasn't the answer I should give. "My brother-in-law just is being sweet." I gave her a tight smile.

"She's doing a great job. Oh, and my mother loved your basket, Kathy. Thanks again." He sipped from his cup.

Slightly mollified, she gave him a bright smile. "Yes, well, I'm glad Melissa liked them. Did you have business with us? Another order, perhaps?"

I looked down and stabbed a bit of baby's breath in the basket of base greens I'd put together. I'd been here barely two weeks and Kathy's cheap ways were starting to grate already. Great.

"Maybe next time. They're still fresh and gorgeous."

"Thanks for the coffee, Gage."

He glanced at me, frowning a little. "Sure. Do you want me to grab you something for lunch?"

"She's still making up her time," Kathy answered for me.

Gage turned and I knew he was going to tell her what happened. I did not want that out there. It was bad enough that people might have seen me faint, but I didn't want this woman looking at me with pity. She'd probably just squish me under her stupid stained Crocs with a sneer.

"I'm fine, Gage. We'll catch up later."

"No, it's not fine. If you had seen her earlier, you wouldn't be giving her crap. I wanted her to stay home and rest, but she was adamant about coming in to work."

"She looks fine. Maybe she was just tired because you two were out partying."

He took a step toward her. "We were not."

"You seem awfully involved for someone who is just her brother-in-law."

"Family takes care of each other."

I swallowed down the flood of warmth at his words. I had family. It wasn't as if I was an orphan or unloved, but my parents weren't exactly the type to get all up in someone's business on my behalf.

"Well, she seems fine. I think you're exaggerating. Now, she has a lot of work to do." Kathy crossed her arms, her face inscrutable.

I grasped his upper arm. "It's fine."

"No, it's not. Who acts like that about their employees?"

"It's really not that big a deal." I tried to drag him back near the door, but he wasn't moving.

"This is the third time she's been late." Kathy sniffed.

This time, he turned to me. "Has this happened before?"

I knew what he was talking about, but Kathy did not. "Let it go."

He frowned down at me and reached out to touch my cheek.

I backed up. Embarrassment flamed up my chest and neck. I hated being put on the spot like this, which was funny since I wasn't exactly the type to downplay reactions to being cornered.

But I needed this job. And while I might not have been wild about Kathy or her judgy, cheap ass ways, I would deal with it until I found something else.

"Have you seen a doctor?"

I shook my head. Sleepwalking and insomnia weren't exactly conditions I wanted to shout out to the world. I'd tried sleeping pills, but those lovely side effects they talked about in the commercial? Yeah, not even close to reality.

They made me way worse.

"Why would you need a doctor?" Kathy came forward.

"I don't need a freaking doctor. I just need everyone to leave me alone about it. I didn't sleep well and overslept because I was...sick."

Yeah, that sounded believable. Not. Maybe if my tone hadn't been so damn uncertain.

"I'm sorry, Rylee, but I don't want liars working for me."

I whirled around. "Kathy, I'm not lying. I just have to get used to being in my new place and a new job. I'll be better, I promise. You won't have to worry about me."

Panic shoved down the warm gooey caramel feeling Gage had created. I'd just moved out on my own. I couldn't lose my job too.

Kathy shook her head. "I don't think this is going to work out."

"No, wait." I threw a narrowed gaze at Gage.

"She doesn't need to work here with someone who doesn't care about their employees."

Kathy's eyes went wide. "How dare you?"

"No. You should be ashamed." Gage stepped forward.

"Do not talk for me, Gage Kramer! I am not your girlfriend or wife or whatever that you feel you need to defend me to this woman."

The words *this woman* dripped with venom. Because my flapping jaws did not care if I had to eat tuna three meals a day.

And I didn't even like tuna.

Kathy's face went red. "I think I'd like you to leave now."

Dammit. My stupid mouth. Couldn't just leave it at defend. Nope, sure couldn't. "You know what? I don't want to work here anyway. That three-hundred-dollar vase looks like something out of a discount bin." I whirled around to Gage. "And you, stop getting into my business!" I stomped over to my workstation and grabbed everything I could see in my blind rage.

Keys.

Air Pods.

Phone.

Favorite mug.

All of it went into my purse.

Gage came up behind me and I elbowed him. "Just go."

"No, you're upset."

I glanced at Kathy, who was standing there with a pissy expression. I couldn't even blame Gage for that sour-lemon face.

Just had to get one last shot at her, didn't you, Rylee?

I growled and slammed out the door.

Gage caught the door so I couldn't even have that satisfaction. Then again, knowing my luck right now, I'd shatter the glass pane.

As it was, I didn't even know if I'd get paid for my time there.

"Dammit."

I rushed down the street.

"Rylee, wait."

"I do not want to talk to you right now."

"You're better than that job, and you know it."

I whirled around to face him and the words log-jammed in my brain. I couldn't even think around my anger. Because yes, I was better than that job, but it was all I had right now.

I let out a whoosh of sound like a growl had a baby with a scream and stalked down the sidewalk toward my apartment. Gage, of course, kept walking behind me, but at least he didn't talk.

Because I was pretty sure I would murder him. And I might even get off in my current mental state.

Did insomnia-induced insanity count as a defense?

We were about to find out.

NINE

SHIT.

I was definitely falling off the leader board in every aspect of my life this week.

I kept a safe distance from Rylee. I'd thought her ability with darts was dangerous—it had nothing on her in full-on anger mode.

Then again, I kinda had gotten her fired.

Fuck.

But she really was so much better than that job. She was smart enough and talented enough to be running her own shop. She didn't have the personality to actually work for anyone. I understood, because I was very much the same.

She stalked across the street, the heels of her boots clicking ominously in that way that only women seemed to be able to do. I dashed after her when she didn't even bother to look both ways to check for oncoming traffic.

"Jesus, woman." I scooped her up and set her down on the sidewalk just as a cyclist zipped by.

Her huge dark eyes were startled, almost on the verge of shock.

"Look, I get that you're mad, but you gotta slow down and think."

"*Think?* Right now, I'm going through four different scenarios that I know of to hide your body. One of them might include that lake." She shoved me back and practically ran down the sidewalk.

What the hell was it with the women in this town and threatening me with murder? I wasn't *that* much of an asshole.

At least I didn't think so.

Luckily, my long legs didn't require the sprinting situation she had going on. I drove fast, I didn't run. However, I did pick up the pace when I saw how close she was to her door. I knew she would not let me upstairs.

I managed to grab the door just as she tried to slam it in my face.

"I did not invite you in."

"Rylee?"

"What?"

"Shut up." I pulled her against my chest and covered her mouth with mine. It was the only way I knew to quiet her down long enough to let me in.

Miraculously, she didn't even pretend to fight me. I knew she was riding that adrenaline wave and needed a target. Instead of stabbing me with whatever sharp implements she could find in her apartment, she allowed me to re-route her agenda.

She went up on her toes and dragged me down closer. "This doesn't mean anything, you understand me?"

"Right. Not a thing." I curled my arm around her waist and hauled her up against me, half carrying her and half dragging her up the stairs.

I slammed my hip into the doorknob as we got to the top of the stairs. Her apartment was the first one on her floor. She reached around me to twist it open and shoved me against the island right inside the door.

Memories of our first night slammed into me. She'd been much the same that night. Determined to find some sort of outlet using me and the crazy attraction that flamed between us.

I'd wanted it to be more that night, and those same feelings were crowding me now. I was the king of one-nighters, but nothing about Rylee felt as if it should be one and done, no matter what she said. And I was going to prove it to her.

But this go-round, I wasn't going to let her make all the rules. We'd tried that before.

It was time for her to see just what—and who—she was dealing with.

I picked her up and set her on the counter, shoving the drainer into the sink. Handily, it was empty.

She went for my pants, but I set her hands on the counter. "Stay there."

Her dark eyes were like burning embers and her chest heaved as if she'd run a mile. She was so goddamn beautiful when she was angry. Evidently, I had issues and I was so totally going down, man.

Hopefully literally, because I needed another taste or five hundred of her.

She narrowed her eyes, then tilted her head. "All right."

I was so fucked. But I was going to earn the crash and burn here.

I dragged down the sweater that was already dipping off her shoulder. I brushed a gentle kiss there and moved up to the dark blue strap of her bra, then to the soft skin leading to her neck.

"Move along, Kramer. This is supposed to be for us to let off some steam. You owe me an orgasm at the very least."

I smiled against her skin. "Patience, huntress. This time, you're the one who needs to settle in and enjoy."

"I enjoyed just fine last time."

I closed my teeth around her earlobe, her earring clicking against the enamel. I tugged and she let out a gasp. I brushed away the soft, wispy hair from her messy knot. I needed all that raven-colored hair around her shoulders.

She lifted her hand to her hair.

"Back where your hands are supposed to be."

"Or what?" But she put her hand back on the counter.

"Or I'll walk out that door and try again."

She hooked her leg around the back of my thigh. "That is not the agreement here."

"You think this is just about scratching an itch. I'm here to show you it's not just a bounce." I ran my nose along her neck. "I want more."

"What, for the few weeks you'll be here? Maybe a month.?"

"You keep talking like you know what my plan is."

"Oh, and like *you* know?"

"Nope. I don't." I eased back so I could look her in the eye. "But I do know that we're both on the edge of something new and different. Why can't we figure it out together? What are you afraid of?"

She lifted her chin. "I'm not afraid of anything. I just know the score."

"You think you do." I lowered my mouth to hers and let the curl of annoyance flow into her. The kiss was hard and soft at the same time. I owned the bit of real estate there. Her soft, full lips were made for mine. She knew just how to give and take. As the greed took us under, I hooked her legs firmly around my hips.

I fumbled with her zipper and she tried to get to my belt. I grabbed her fingers and set them back on the edge of the counter. Apparently, asking her to keep her hands there was too much. "There, huntress. Give me just a few more minutes, and then you can rip into me."

"You make me sound like a freaking animal." She dropped her head back as I went for her throat again.

"I remember the claw marks I wore for days after you left me."

She groaned as my fingers pushed through the layers of cotton, silk, and lace to find what I'd been longing for. The sweet, warm cleft I still dreamed about on the lonely nights.

I twisted my wrist to slowly sink two fingers into her. She hissed and lifted to my touch. God, she drove me crazy with just how much she owned her sexuality. Most women would need a few drinks to be this free. Then it was just sloppy and a totally different experience.

I couldn't say I hadn't enjoyed a few of those nights in my time, but this...

This was pure Rylee.

She rolled her hips in time with my touch. My name a whispered sigh rumbling in her chest and teasing her tongue. I wanted the first crack at it. Not to let it free to the air, but to own it and swallow it inside me.

She didn't want to know my name that first night, but now it tumbled out of her like breath. She strained under my orders for her hands to stay at her sides. If she touched me, I'd be done. I wouldn't be able to deny her anything.

Again.

Like then, but even stronger now because I knew what she was like and I was running into that storm with knowledge and hopefully, a little more fortitude.

Each burning groan I took and gave back more with a flick of my thumb to add to the grasping tightness of her pussy. My forearm ached and spasmed at the angle, but I didn't care. She was going to come with my name on her fucking lips.

I curved deeper and thrust slowly and endlessly as she gasped and shifted against me. I dragged the other shoulder of her sweater down with the strap of her little scrap of lace under the sweater.

Her little brown nipple puckered, and I covered it, sucking on it hard as she bucked up for more. "Yes," I mumbled against her skin.

Warm silk over the most perfect breasts on the damn planet.

I cupped my hand around it, lifting so I could get to every bit of her. I relearned her taste and with each flick of my tongue, she arched for me. Finally, she cried out and shook around my hand, her arm hooking around my neck to hold me tighter to her breast.

My name was a shout with a desperate groan chaser.

Shit, I couldn't wait any longer.

I slid out of her and wrapped my arms around her. "Hold onto me."

Once her legs and arms were secure around my shoulders and hips, I strode through her tiny living room to the doorway of her bedroom. I set her down on the twisted sheets and we both stripped. My fingers were shaking, for fuck's sake.

I was still trying to open my button-down shirt when she flipped her sweater over her head and went for my belt.

I groaned as she curled her fingers around my shaft and gave it a firm squeeze. "God, do that again," I said on a broken breath.

She stood up and fisted my cock with a wild smirk. "Get inside me and I'll squeeze you even tighter."

"Jesus."

I toed off my boots and eased her away from me so I could get my goddamn jeans and underwear off. I had just enough brain power left to dig out my wallet and a condom before I threw my jeans to the side.

However, Rylee would not be deterred. She twisted her long fingers between my arms and got a hold of me again.

I tossed the condom on her bedside table. Since she wasn't going to listen to me at this point, I shifted and went for her jeans instead. She kicked off her boots with a little help from me, and we both rolled onto her bed with a laugh.

My only goal was to get inside her perfect pussy.

I knelt between her legs and swiped my thumb up her soaked slit. She rolled her hips as she circled my wrist to bring the flat pad of my thumb back down where she needed it. She hissed out a breath as I found her clit.

I wanted inside her, to feel the clasp of her body again. But I knew I wasn't going to last.

There hadn't been anyone since Rylee.

Even when I attempted to push her out of my head with another woman, I couldn't get beyond a drink. Hell, I hadn't even kissed anyone since her.

She was a first for me in so many ways.

I lowered my mouth to the little triangle of dark hair and sipped from her soaked skin. I found her clit and lightly curled my tongue around it and explored my way to every pleasure center she had. She pushed at my head to get me to stop, but I wasn't going to be happy until I heard my name again.

I sucked and twirled my tongue around her tight little clit. To get some relief, I pressed my throbbing hard-on into the bed. Concentrating on her was what mattered now.

I could wait. I *would* wait.

She raked her nails over the nape of my neck, then down to my shoulders as she went up and over again. Her thighs quivered and she sobbed out nonsensical words. Her head thrashed on the pillows, scattering them onto the floor as she tried to twist away from me. When I wouldn't let her, she held on to the white wooden headboard and swore she'd kill me.

I didn't stop.

Couldn't.

I wanted to laugh and tell her to just try and get me off of her right now, but my brain was Swiss cheese with the need to bury myself inside her.

I wanted to demand my name, but I needed her to give it even more.

She dug her heels into the mattress and lifted her hips to my mouth as I drank her down. I flattened my hand over her soft belly and joined my thumb in the torture with my tongue.

Finally, she cried out my name and I nearly sagged in relief.

But instead of letting her think for a minute we were even close to done, I rolled onto my knees and gently folded her legs together. The gorgeous curve of her hip drew my mouth like a flame.

I bit the rounded curve of her truly excellent ass. She curled her knees up against her chest, but that wasn't what I was after.

Though part of me thought about sliding between her tucked legs and letting her strangle my cock with each thrust.

But I wouldn't last.

I knew I wouldn't. And I was prideful enough to dig deep for a little more strength.

I reached for the condom and cursed my shaking hands as I rolled it on. When I looked up again, Rylee was kneeling facing away from me, her hands on the headboard.

"I'm not done with you yet."

"Fuck."

She lifted her ass in invitation. "That would be the plan." She looked over her shoulder and I closed my eyes on a silent prayer that this wasn't the last time I'd get to do this.

I tugged her down lower and brushed the tip of my dick along her swollen pussy. She rotated her hips slowly and took me inside.

I tipped my head back as I slowly sunk into her. If I watched, it would be over. She was molten heat and gripped me so tightly. Each inch I slid deeper made me feel huge and powerful. I curved my hands around her hips and eased out of her, praying the whimper in my head didn't come out of my mouth. Then I snapped my hips forward and buried myself back into her perfection.

She pushed back on me, shifting the angle, and her head fell between her braced arms as we lost ourselves in the relentless rhythm of pure, animal fucking. I took and she gave. I drove into her and she demanded more.

But it was never, ever enough.

Sweat poured between us and the air went blue with both of us demanding the other fuck harder, take everything.

She rose onto her knees, letting go of the headboard to reach back for me. Then she used my thighs as a lever to drive herself up and down. All that wild dark hair flew in my face, drowning me in her rich, earthy scent. Plants, flowers, and just pure Rylee, whole and untamed.

Christ, she was going to make me lose it.

As if she'd heard my thoughts, her nails sliced into my skin as we crashed onto our sides. I lifted her leg up to get deeper again. She was wide open to me and my fingers. I raced up from her clit to her belly and nipples, then back down.

"Just come, for fuck's sake," she cried out and grabbed my hand, dragging it down to her clit. "I'm so close. Just…God, Gage."

I pumped inside of her and it was as if she'd said the magic words. Who knew my name would be the gateway to nirvana?

She did somehow. She'd figured out my secret, the thing I needed most from her.

Exactly *this.*

I held her tight to me and thrust deep. Her fingers covered mine as we both circled her tight clit.

She finally curled into herself, shaking around my trapped hand. I dug one arm under her and crowded into her with the other as I finally let go into the condom, wishing it wasn't between us at all.

I buried my face into her neck and her name was my ultimate prayer.

I barely had the wherewithal to take care of the condom before we both drifted off with the late day sun striping across us.

"Gage."

I rolled over, curling my arm around her waist. "Later."

"You gotta go."

"Later." I buried my face in her hair. It smelled so delicious. Like we'd fucked in the rainforest after dancing naked in the rain.

Yeah, I needed a nap.

"No, you have to go now. I need to get some sleep."

I rubbed my chin along her shoulder. "Comfy bed. We'll both sleep. I don't care if you snore."

"I do not snore!"

Her outrage sounded suspiciously like the same tone she'd used when she found out she'd fainted in front of me. "Okay then, even better."

"I like to sleep alone."

I lifted my head. "Is that why you kicked me out last time?"

I'd thought that was more of a dude thing. Personally, I enjoyed a good cuddle. It did the body good. Unless it was over eighty degrees, then I needed to revise that thought.

Then again, I'd never really stuck around for much more than a Sunday morning hangover cuddle.

But Rylee was different. I liked her smell—obviously—and the way she leaned into me.

Pretty much everything was an anomaly when it came to her.

My eyes were already closing again. "I'll leave in a few minutes."

She shook my shoulder. "Gotta go now."

I propped myself up on my elbow. "What the hell, Ry?"

"You knew what this was when you came upstairs with me." She sat up against the headboard, her arm holding the sheet up against her breasts.

"Yes, but that doesn't mean we can't have a little afternoon catnap." I tugged on the sheet with a grin.

She pulled it up more firmly. "It's been a long day."

I sat up and swung my legs off the bed. Even I could take a hint eventually. "Yes, it has been. I thought it had been a good one in the end."

"I'm still jobless. I just happened to get a few more orgasms as a severance package."

"Wow. Thanks, glad to help." I stood up and grabbed my jeans and underwear before closing myself in the small bathroom outside her bedroom.

I took care of business and got dressed, then washed my hands and got my shit under control before I came back out.

I'd known when I came upstairs with her that she was going to do this. I'd hoped she wouldn't, but I shouldn't be surprised. It wasn't as if she was acting differently from the last time we'd been together.

But dammit, it all *felt* different. The night before the wedding, it had been a regular hookup. I'd appreciated the fact that she didn't want to linger and make things weird.

I curled my hands around the sides of her tiny sink. Now?

Now, it felt as if she was simply shutting me out for no good reason. I knew I wasn't a good bet, but I wasn't a fucking ogre.

Not even close.

I opened the door and went back into her bedroom. She was laying on her side, her back to me. She'd pulled on an oversized T-shirt that dwarfed her and put the bed back together from pillows to blankets.

The sheets were the same color, or I'd have said she stripped the bed to erase me. Maybe all hope wasn't lost if she wanted to smell me on her sheets for a little longer. But fuck, she looked so small and almost sad. And dammit, I didn't want that either.

The anger seeped out of me. Clearly, more was going on here than

I'd suspected. Maybe she had bad shit in her past that made her wary about trusting men.

I picked up my shirt that she'd neatly set at the end of the bed. I'd just have to work a little harder to prove to her that I was worth a chance.

TEN

I STARED OUT THE WINDOW AS GAGE QUIETLY GOT DRESSED AND LEFT my room. I ached to tell him to stay. To feel his arms around me again.

I understood sex. I wasn't one of those women who pretended that it wasn't one of the best things God ever invented on the little rock we called home. Procreation aside, it was a damn fine way to spend a day.

And Gage was generous and inventive without looking for me to do some yoga pose he saw in the Kama Sutra. His freaking tongue should be bronzed—twice, then put in some hall of fame. Secretly, of course, because he didn't need a bigger head about it.

Though the head at the end of his cock certainly held cause for standing ovations. Jesus, that man knew how to make my body sing.

The part about him making my body sing, I could deal with. It was the sleeping together business that caused me to pause. I could have curled right into a long, lovely nap. His body was warm without being a furnace, which was definitely a problem in my life lately.

If menopause meant hot flashes like the ones I was having, I was not looking forward to my later years.

But the idea of him finding about my sleepwalking? And the possibility of doing something crazy in front of him?

No, no, with a side of hell no. I just couldn't allow him to see me that way. He'd think I was a freak. Maybe I was.

I slid my pillow over my head.

Never again. My boyfriend in college had found out stress equaled zombie Rylee. And at first, Shane had been super sweet about it. Only teased me a little about my odd little quirks. But when I'd ended up in the middle of the quad at two in the morning—yeah, it had stopped being cute. Especially since there was a party going on that night.

He became known for having the weird girlfriend. And that wouldn't do.

I'd been horrified, and embarrassed. Add in the fear factor about wandering somewhere on campus and insomnia destroying my class schedule, and well, college hadn't been for me.

After a few months at home, it had stopped happening. I'd settled into a regular life with a few different jobs over the years. Nothing ever stuck. I'd played around with doing online classes to get a degree, but the whole college experience had been so tainted that eventually, I'd decided to avoid all of it.

I rolled onto my back and pulled the pillow off my face.

God, I didn't want to go back to being that scared, insecure girl. I hated that this was encroaching on my newfound freedom.

Exhaustion sat on me, but I still couldn't settle. And Gage had wrung me out so I should be in a near-coma. A single tear slid down my temple into my hair as I shut my eyes and counted backward with long slow breaths.

If I could just sleep, then maybe I could make sense of my life.

A girl could dream.

I must've dozed off, because when I rolled over again, my room was dark. I stumbled out of bed and used the bathroom and because I actually felt achy, I took a long, hot shower.

Maybe it would put me back to sleep.

I was hungry, but too tired to actually fix anything, so I returned to my bed and surfed the internet on my phone. Soon enough, I was drifting off again. The sun was shining the next time I opened my eyes.

Nothing looked amiss in my bedroom. Halle-freaking-lujah.

I went about my morning ritual even though I didn't have a job to go to. After I brushed my teeth and got dressed, I braved my living room and my belly filled with dread.

My aloe plant sat in the middle of my couch, wearing marshmallows on the ends of each leaf.

"Well, at least I didn't leave my apartment." I said to the room at large as I picked off each fluffy square.

At least I hoped I hadn't.

I hadn't done a grocery run after my last sleep snafu, but the mere thought of doing that right now put me in a deeper funk.

I dumped the marshmallows in the garbage and took a water from the fridge since that was safe. I stacked the cups from my counter in front of the door, made sure the chain was engaged—though that hadn't stopped me before—and returned to my bedroom.

I kicked off my jeans and crawled back under the covers.

Fuck everything and everyone.

The buzz of texts on my phone dented my sleep, but I was too depressed to answer my sister or Gage. I binge-watched *Revenge* and my dreams were filled with water and murder. Probably not the smartest move on my part. I didn't need my subconscious to do any further damage to the outside world.

The cups I'd stacked in front of my door were still there two days later, so at least whatever havoc I wrecked was limited to my apartment. So far, Emily and Victoria's vindictive antics on the show were staying off the playing field of my home. However, my obsession with peanut butter was evidently at an all-time high.

When I couldn't stand my own company any longer, I finally crept downstairs to Brewed Awakening. It had been a few days since I'd kicked Gage out of my place. My version of coffee couldn't compete with the espresso machine of glory in Macy's café.

"Well, hello, stranger."

I turned to find Macy up on a ladder, hanging a pastel swag of bats and pumpkins. I quickly crossed to her when one of the ladder's feet thumped with her monkey stretch. "Jeez. Can't ask for help or something?"

She grinned down at me and looped the little ring around a tiny hidden hook in the corner of one of her built-in shelves. "Why?"

I rolled my eyes. Why indeed. "Well, I'm bored so I can help if you want."

She winged up one of her crazy arched brows. Everything about her features were sharp. Kinda matched her personality. "I haven't seen you in a few days. Can you hand me those pink pumpkins?"

"Yeah. Drama follows me around." I blew out a breath and handed her the brightly glossed gourds. "Your idea of spring is cool."

"Thanks. I'd have the place decked out for Halloween all year round if I didn't have to deal with Whitaker and her cronies."

"Who are they?"

"Town council. They like the classic town decor." She made slow, deliberate quotation marks with her fingers.

"Oh. Yeah, that doesn't surprise me. I bet they have a set day to change over the lights in the gazebo too."

"You know that they do."

"So, pink pumpkins." I laughed.

"Damn right." She tucked a pink pumpkin behind the yellow gourd already on the shelf. Then flipped out two of the Stephen King books on the shelf. Spring meets "It" and "The Stand".

"I love it and the two-finger salute."

"This is why we get along, mocha." She stepped down. "I resisted the urge to send Mrs. Irene Whitaker a very lifelike bat for Christmas."

"I don't even know this woman and I probably would have paid to see it."

"She's friends with your boss."

My smile fell. "Kathy?"

"Yeah." Macy tightened her ever-present ponytail. "Best friends, I'd wager."

"Well, then I definitely would have paid to see that. Ex-boss, by the way."

"That sounds like a story. Want your usual?"

"I would love a coffee."

"You got it." She strode though the café, weaving around tables, picking up mugs and plates on her way through with an efficiency that made me tired.

I'd only been awake for a few hours and it felt as if I was slogging through molasses mid-freeze. And because I was tired of feeling useless, I grabbed a few plates on my way to the counter.

"Thanks, mocha."

Suddenly, Macy's face was being eaten by black dots. Plates hit the floor and the last thing I saw was Macy's "oh, shit" face before the room went lights out.

Next thing I knew, Macy and Vee were propping me up on the couch.

"All right, there she is." Macy's face swam into focus.

Vee held a cool washcloth on my neck.

I shook my head. "Oh, no."

"You scared the crap out of us, mocha. I'm thinking this isn't the first time based on the look on your face."

"Oh, shit." I dropped my face into my hands. "What the hell is going on?" Tears threatened, but I managed to battle them back. Crying wouldn't help.

Macy stood and went to the front counter. "She's fine, people. Go back to your food." She grabbed a bottle of water and came back to sit next to me.

"This is bottled water. Because you don't drink the water in Crescent Cove. Unless it's too late." She held the bottle away from me. "Did you?"

"What? No. I..." I shook my head. "No."

"Really? Because Gage was up at your place for a while the other day," Vee said with a grin.

"Yeah, well, even his super sperm isn't good enough to inseminate me in two freaking days."

"That's true. Maybe you just have a virus." Vee stood up, then rubbed my arm. "You okay?"

No. I was so very far away from okay, but I waved her off. "Yes, sorry. Go ahead and do your thing."

Vee glanced at Macy, then at me with barely concealed glee. "More babies."

"I'm not pregnant," I whispered.

"You sure about that?" She collapsed back on the couch next to me.

"Of course. I haven't done anything…like that."

Macy and Vee exchanged knowing glances while my mind spun.

Except for that crazy night in December when Gage and I were so insane for each other. We'd practically fallen on each other as if we hadn't had sex for years. And okay, it had been awhile for me, but I still couldn't explain it. Even after another round with him, I couldn't begin to understand why I reacted to him like I did.

Like he was oxygen and I was starving for it.

And that first night?

We'd been insatiable.

Much like the second go-round. If he'd stayed for that nap he wanted to take, I had no doubt that afterward, we would've been playing naked bingo with his dick for a chip.

Or a dauber. Jeez, what did they play bingo with nowadays anyway?

Not penises, that was for sure. Missed opportunity.

"That's not a good expression," Macy said.

I frowned. I didn't even have cause for alarm. I mean, I didn't have the most reliable period, but I'd definitely remember not having it for freaking months. "No, I got my period since…well, the last time I—" I huffed out a breath. "Not that you need to know all that."

Macy crossed her arms and tucked herself into the corner of the couch. "I don't know much about the baby thing, but there's all sorts of mysteries during pregnancy. This fucking town is way too much of an education."

"Yeah, but I used protection. There's no way."

"No way, what?"

I nearly choked at the deep voice behind me. *Please God, no.*

All dogs might go to heaven, but all Rylees perpetually lived in hell.

Maybe that was just me.

Macy's eyes widened and she popped off the couch. "Yep, my cue to go."

"Wimp," I growled.

"Yes, ma'am. And I just remembered I need to order filters for all the machines."

Vee laughed and hurried after her boss.

"Assholes," I muttered, but a laugh bubbled under the word. Maybe Macy really was onto something when it came to this town.

"Filters? Did I miss something?" Gage looked down at me and immediately crouched in front of me. "God, you're pale." His eyes narrowed. "Shit. Did you faint again?"

I wanted to die. I still replayed that moment when Gage had lifted me into his arms far too often. Embarrassment warred with pleasure that he cared about my well-being. Then and now, judging from the worry lines dug deep into his forehead.

Even his forehead was hot. Or else I was a touch feverish to go with my fainting spells and exhaustion.

I was a bag of fun, except not even close.

"No...yes. Maybe."

"Ah, huntress. We need to get you to a doctor. What happens if it's something more serious than you not sleeping?"

It seemed that it might be way more serious and no pill could fix me. Well, not anymore.

Reflexively, I covered my middle with my hand. I couldn't be pregnant. Wouldn't I have other signs...

Oh, like hormones going crazy maybe?

Like eating everything in sight, even when I was technically unconscious?

Perhaps feeling as if a bus had hit me without tapping the brakes, sleep or no sleep?

Nope, no signs at all.

He took my hand. "Are you feeling sick?"

God, could this get any worse?

"Gage, I'm okay."

My affliction might be of the nine-month variety. With an extra special bonus of something that will be a part of me forever.

I met his gaze. *Part of us.*

Just the thought of us forever linked made my brain whirl.

If I was pregnant—which was still a very strong *if*—my baby daddy was a race car driver without a job right now. He probably wouldn't even be sticking around.

I had no job. And no idea what the hell I was doing. Oh, and I was sleepwalking again.

My free hand went to my middle. "What if I hurt the—" I swallowed.

Saying the word would make it real. I wasn't ready to go there yet.

"Hurt the—" His eyebrows snapped down. "Are you pregnant?"

Honesty was the only thing I had left. I was simply too tired to even try to evade.

"I don't know."

ELEVEN

If the floor opened up and swallowed me whole, I couldn't have been more surprised.

"Rylee."

"I don't know, Gage. Okay?" Her huge dark eyes were wild. She kept looking around the room. Anywhere but at me. And her hand crept along her belly.

Jesus.

Part of her and part of me in there.

"Mine?"

Finally, her eyes stopped wheeling around. "Of course it's yours." She stood up and pushed me back. "Who else? I don't go around doing —what we did with just anyone."

I caught myself on the edge of the table and straightened from my crouched position. "Okay, okay. I just had to ask."

"Which is exactly why I wouldn't want to tell you."

"You wouldn't what?"

She tried to walk out of the room, but I caught her wrist. "You wouldn't tell me?"

"I don't know." She tugged her wrist free.

My gut bottomed out again. "I get that you're upset, but Jesus, Rylee. It's our kid we're talking about."

"Keep your voice down."

"Because you're ashamed to have my kid?" I didn't lower my voice. Sure enough, people started glancing our way.

"No. I didn't say that."

"Oh, really? Because that's what it sounds like."

"Tell me something. Would you be here right now if you weren't bored? Wouldn't you be on some racetrack in Florida or God knows where?"

"Daytona already happened."

"I don't know the races, Gage. Pick another one. Any one that you would be at this spring and summer." Her eyes flashed and her hands fisted at her sides.

"Would you have told me?"

The fact that I had to ask her made my chest ache. Would she really keep it from me?

"Since I literally just thought of it, I can't answer that."

"I think you just did."

"What do you want me to say?" She sliced her hand through the air. "We were together once."

"Twice," I reminded her.

"And neither time was supposed to mean anything serious."

"Maybe not to you."

The anger knitting her brows cleared into shock. "What?"

I tried to control the fear and anger growing in my chest. I'd already been wound up about her kicking me out the other day. I couldn't stop thinking about her and for once, it wasn't only because I was using the wrong head.

She was exciting and intelligent, and her mouth made me nuts. Not just when it came to kissing her or tasting her, but the crazy things she said. But the idea that she could be having my kid...

Everything stilled inside of me.

Maybe I was being given a second chance after all. All the money in the world didn't mean anything when I was always alone. Passing the time with a pretty girl had been fun for a long time, but only because there'd been nothing but winning burning in my brain.

Meeting Rylee that day at The Spinning Wheel had jarred something loose inside of me. Something I didn't even realize I needed.

Someone who meant more than a sweaty night.

Maybe she didn't see me as anything more than that. And that was the real problem. I needed to prove to her that I could be counted on.

"Even if there's no baby, I'm not just looking for a hot fuck anymore."

"What?"

Her startled glance told me I was on the right path. I stepped closer to her, curling my arm around her back. She was too surprised to back up right away. When she tensed, I cupped her cheek. "I've been trying to tell you since I got back to town that I want to spend time with you."

"Yes, I know what you want."

"You don't. I mean, of course I want *this.*" I yanked her closer so she could see what she did to me just by being in the same room. "But I'm also not a fourteen-year-old led around by my dick."

"As you push your hard-on into me."

"He wants you."

"It's sentient?" She rested her hand on my chest, but she wasn't pushing me back this time.

"Let's just say he's had a mind of his own in the past. But you're not alone in this, Ry. Not by a long shot. And if you don't want me—" I cleared my throat and resisted the urge to toss her over my shoulder and prove just how much that was a lie. "I'll respect it. I'll keep trying to change your mind, but I'll respect it."

She broke our gaze. "Gage—"

"Let me finish."

Her dark eyes lifted to mine again.

"I want to be in my baby's life. Just know I want the mom too."

She lifted her chin. "And if there's no baby?"

"Maybe you'll want one with me someday."

Her eyes shimmered. "You don't even know me."

"You're worth getting to know. I've survived this long by following my instincts." I lowered my mouth to hers. "So, maybe don't give up on me yet," I whispered against her mouth before giving her the kind of kiss she wouldn't soon forget.

If she wanted to push me away again, I'd let her this time. Because in the kiss was a touch of salt and it broke me in a way I didn't know what to do with.

"Ah, babe." I pressed my forehead to hers. "We'll figure it out together."

"Okay."

I didn't realize I was holding my breath until she said that single word. "How about we go see if we have anything to worry about?"

She nodded. "Yeah."

I framed her face with my hands. "Just one question."

Her lashes were starred with tears, but they weren't running down her face. Small mercies. "Yes?"

"If there is a baby, do you want it?"

"Yes."

I closed my eyes. No hesitation. I swallowed down the lump that had been climbing up with each minute since she'd dropped the bomb on me. I opened my eyes when she wrapped her fingers around my wrists. "Good."

"Just let me go wash my face and get my purse."

I nodded. "I'll be here." Letting her go alone was a lesson in patience and I really sucked at that particular virtue.

"Not bad, ace."

I glanced over at Macy. She was leaning against the half wall sectioning off the café with the couches and comfortable reading nook she'd created. "Thanks, I think."

"I was mostly kidding when I mentioned it to her, but then a few things started adding up." She chewed on the inside of her cheek.

"Got something else to say?"

"Just go easy on her. I like her." She drummed her fingers on the half wall. "I don't like too many people. So, just remember I've got a really big baseball bat and lots and lots of—"

"Solvents. Yes, I'm aware."

"I like a guy who listens." She headed back to her counter. "I made you a coffee and her a hot chocolate." She glanced over her shoulder. "Just in case."

I had to laugh. Damned if I didn't like Macy too.

By the time I got back to the reading nook with our drinks, Rylee was back. She had on a different shirt and a little makeup. I passed her the hot cocoa, then held out my hand for her. She hesitated for only a moment before wrapping her fingers around mine.

"I'm assuming you want to go out of town."

"God, yes."

"I figured." I took a quick sip of my coffee. Still glorious.

She peered at my cup. "Why does mine say hot chocolate?"

"I guess Macy is up on this baby stuff. No coffee."

"None?" Her jaw fell open.

"Pretty limited, from what I've heard from Dare. Guess you'll be able to talk to your sister about it."

"How am I going to tell my parents I'm having a baby and I lost my job in the same week?"

"One step at a time."

"Right." She nodded and went through the door ahead of me.

"I can take care of us."

She glanced back at me. "I don't need you to take care of me. Of us."

"I know."

"I lost my job, but I have savings."

I circled her wrist gently to stop her from walking ahead. "I think you're the most capable woman I know."

"We've established you don't know me all that well." She shook me off and folded both hands around her cup. If I wasn't mistaken, her fingers were trembling.

"And I'll continue to get to know you, but I'm used to strong women. I wouldn't be attracted to you if you weren't." When she wrinkled her nose at me, I knew I had her. "No argument there, huh?"

She started walking and I lengthened my stride to match hers. "Mine's the dark gray one."

"A dick car?" She frowned at me. "I know for a fact you aren't lacking in that department."

"Thanks. Somehow you know just how to make a compliment sound like an insult."

"It's a gift."

I held the door open for her. "More like Chevys are comfortable for me."

She got in and looked up at me. "I don't remember race cars looking like this."

"Well, I still like a good motor." I grinned, then shut the door. The Stingray was an indulgence. I was still driving a rental since my Camaro had died a pathetic death in Colorado. Evidently, I would have to start thinking about something more in tune with my future. I got in on the driver's side. "It's a rental."

She looked around at the tight quarters. "Can't deny the hotness factor."

I revved the engine. "No, ma'am."

She let out a surprised laugh when I pulled out onto Main. I had to keep it under thirty, but when I got to the turnoff for the next town over, I opened it up a little.

It felt good to drive again, but I was also conscious of precious cargo for the first time in my life.

I was a very good driver—one of the safest in the industry—but for once, I wasn't looking to impress someone with my skills. I wanted to make sure I got us safely where we needed to go.

There were a few towns surrounding Crescent Cove. I didn't really want to head into my old stomping grounds either.

It was bad enough people knew me on sight. I could walk into a room and usually no one could place me, but at the same time, I was noticed. And all it took was one whisper. I didn't want the tabloids screaming about me and a woman getting a pregnancy test when we hadn't even brought up the subject with our families.

A few minutes later, I pulled into the parking lot of a small CVS. "So, there's just one problem."

"Just one?"

I scrubbed my palms on my thighs. "I'm going to sound like an asshole. And I don't want you to go in there alone."

She crossed her arms. "You just said we were in this together. So, that changed in three miles? Nice."

I turned in my seat. "I'd go in there and clear them out of pregnancy tests. I don't care about that. But what if someone recognizes me?"

She stared out the window with her jaw set. "Oh, big bad race car driver knocked up a chick?"

Gently, I gripped her chin and turned her face toward me. "More like heading number three on US Weekly's email list. 'Gage Kramer and gorgeous stranger buy pregnancy test.' Not sure about you, but those things get talked about in our circles." She narrowed her gaze. "By our parents and friends, never mind anyone else."

"Oh."

"Yeah, oh."

I pulled out my wallet and counted out a few hundred dollars.

"Gage, they're not that expensive."

I just gave her the whole wad of bills. "Buy what you think you need and come back to me."

She sighed. "Why do you have to surprise me?"

I laughed. "Gotta keep things interesting, right?" She opened her door, but before she could get out, I dragged her back against me and covered her mouth with mine. The kiss was far too quick. "Thanks."

She licked her lips and gave me another quizzical look. "I'll be right back."

I tapped on the steering wheel and checked my phone.

Over and over again.

How the hell long did it take to buy a test? Or a few tests. The parking lot had only a handful of cars.

Fuck it, I was going to get out and check on her. For God's sake, what if she'd fainted again?

She opened the door and got in with the telltale white and red bag. "Sorry. I wasn't sure what to buy. I looked online for the best test and then there were so many different options online, and in the store." She huffed out a breath and shoved the bills back at me. "I got three different ones that were the highest rated."

"All right then." When I tried to wave off the money, she growled.

I wasn't winning that battle. It was better to wave the white flag there. I tucked the wad into my jeans pocket and pulled out. "Where do we want to do this?"

"My place, I guess."

I nodded.

She pulled out each box and read the back of them as she chewed on the side of her thumbnail.

"Is it hard?"

"Doesn't seem like it. Pee on the stick and wait for the lines or the words to come up. I got both kinds."

"Right."

We parked near her building and went in the side entrance and up the stairs. She dropped the bag on the island and started ripping into the boxes.

I glanced at the stack of peach cups on her counter. "Lots of cups. Need any water? You know, to—"

Her gaze darted from the cups to me, then back again. "Um, no. I'm good." She cleared her throat. "I'll be right back."

"Right. Okay." I popped my knuckles and paced her small living room.

She came back out a few minutes later, drying her hands on a hand towel. "We have to wait like three minutes and five minutes for one."

I looked down at my watch and set my timer. "The longest five minutes of my life."

"We can check in three."

"But then if they're all done, we'll know for sure."

"Smart. Not sure how you can wait that long, but you know, we can."

I went to her and grasped her hands. "Do you feel...different?"

"Considering I was shocked when Macy put this stupid idea in my head? Yeah, I'm going to say no."

I played with her fingers. "Stupid question."

"How do you think it happened? If, you know, we are."

I resisted the urge to smile. She'd said *we,* not I. It was the little things. "All I can figure is when we got into the hotel and you jumped me. I wasn't thinking and you felt so fucking good that even after I came, I was still hard and kept..." I blew out a breath. "Every guy knows to pull out after you finish so something stupid doesn't happen, but I wasn't fucking thinking."

"You do have amazing resiliency."

"Thanks, I think."

She shook her head. "God. Has it been three minutes?"

"Five, remember?"

"At three, we can start."

"No, five, then we know for certain."

She closed her eyes and shook out her hands. "You are much too calm about this."

Surprisingly, I was. Because nothing had ever felt so right in my life.

When my watch beeped, Rylee ran to the bathroom. I followed and at her gasp, I smiled.

She came out with three wands in her hand. She glanced up at me, her huge dark eyes larger than I'd ever seen them. "Every single one says yes."

I picked her up and swung her around. "We're having a baby." I dropped a kiss on her shocked mouth.

"Holy crap, I guess we are."

TWELVE

The best way to deal with something was to rip the Band-Aid off. Or so I'd heard. So, I'd chosen the smaller Band-Aid to attack first.

Sister reveal, then parents, then the town at large.

God, if ever I'd needed alcohol, this was it. But nope, I was officially a teetotaler until I birthed my young.

Childbirth.

I couldn't even keep a job for two weeks lately, but I could parent a newborn. Sure. No big.

After a brief talk about this pregnancy not being a crisis—ha, lies—I'd sent Gage home and promptly fallen asleep on the couch. Unaided, without any apps. And I hadn't moved for the better part of six hours.

When I awakened, I'd found a text from Gage.

Just checking on the mom-to-be. Hope you're resting.

I'd rolled my eyes, but I couldn't help smiling a little too. Probably dopily. And I'd even answered him without much delay, mentioning I was fine and craving a sandwich.

I can go pick it up. Do you like corned beef, ham, turkey? Oh, there's nitrates. Aren't those bad for babies? I saw something on the news. Maybe a veggie sandwich is best.

I'd given him a mental middle finger at that one and said no, thanks. Why go for deli meat when I could have my old faithful peanut butter?

At this point, I wasn't far from scraping the bottom of the jar. I might have to invest in a bulk order of the stuff.

My baby would probably have a nut-shaped head.

Full from my sandwich—okay, two sandwiches—I'd dozed again without incident. It was a damn miracle. Probably even my dazed brain couldn't marshal enough forces to manage to sleepwalk while in the throes of such life-changing news.

So, now I was pressing my luck at my sister's place. We were meeting with her friends in a little while to discuss all things baby shower, so what better time to tell Kel that I'd also imbibed the Crescent Cove baby juice?

It probably actually wasn't a good time. These preparations should be all about her, not me. But I supposed I needed some comfort from someone who understood what it was like to be invaded without an invitation.

Or else attention-grabbing little sister syndrome was kicking in once again. Though I wouldn't have minded skipping center stage when it came to this.

I played with the donkey-shaped salt and pepper shakers on Kelsey and Dare's kitchen table.

Rather appropriate, because I felt like an ass.

"Do you want some decaf tea? Oh, no, of course not." Kelsey thunked herself in the forehead with the heel of her hand. "I forget not everyone is on a restricted diet. I won't be either soon. Soon as this guy takes flight," she patted her enormous belly, "I'll probably drown myself in caffeine."

"I thought you were iffy on coffee to begin with?"

"Macy taught me her Jedi ways. Or is it Yoda? I never can get that straight." She waved her hand. "Anyway, her coffee is bomb. Have you tried it?"

I blinked at my sister. "Excuse me, did you just say current lingo?"

Kelsey grinned and lifted the whistling teapot off the stove and poured the tea into a fussy china cup. "The kids say the craziest things. Best part is trying to vex Dare with the newest stuff I've learned. He usually adopts whatever it is within a few days."

Now I knew I was hearing things. "Surly Dare cares about being current?"

"Dare isn't surly. He just seems that way sometimes. No, he doesn't care about being current. But somehow it seems to sneak into his vocabulary. Probably the married thing. Next thing you know, I'll be talking about spark plugs." She looked over her shoulder and wrinkled her freckled nose. "No, probably not."

I ran my fingertip over the donkey's tail. "Do you ever wonder what you missed out on?"

"Huh?"

"Like, you know, in life. You only ever dated that loser Tommy and then you came here, and in no time, you were shackled to Dare and squeezing out a kid. You never got to really party."

"Me? Party?" Kelsey laughed. "My idea of a party is crocheting baby hats while watching *The Great British Baking Show.* When I get really wild, Sage and Ally come over to make fun of the show and we drink hot cocoa."

"You're pretty tight with them now, huh?"

Kelsey carried her teacup to the table. "Yeah, I am. It's awesome. I always wanted girlfriends. The kind who just get you and make you laugh, and you can say anything to. You know what I mean?"

I started to answer. I even had a good reply in my head.

Yes. That's sweet. I'm glad that you have that in your life now. You deserve it.

Instead, I began blubbering.

Kelsey frowned and paused with her teacup halfway to her mouth. "Ry? What are you—is that—oh my God, you're crying. I didn't think you could."

Through my tears, I choked out a laugh. "What?"

"I always thought you'd been born without tear ducts."

That was the impression I liked to give off. So much for that right now. "Surprise."

Kelsey made a soft noise of distress and waddled around the table to stroke my hair. I'd braided it to get it out of my face, so she couldn't do much more than pat, but even that helped. "I heard about the job. Don't fret. Kathy is a stone-cold bitch."

It was my turn to goggle. My sister never said stuff like that about people. She was the sweet one. I was the…not sweet one. "How did you find out?"

Kelsey waved off the question. "Small town. You know how it is."

Even considering where I'd grown up, Crescent Cove was its own kind of beast. I was learning the hard way.

"But you can find something else. They're always looking for people down at the school. Oh!" She clapped her hands as if she was bringing her classroom to order. "Just last week, the receptionist gave her notice. You're great with filing."

"My nails?"

"No, silly. You've had secretarial jobs before."

I had, but not many and not for long. Though that covered my job history in full. I was out almost as fast as I was in. "Yes. But at a school? Especially a Catholic school? I'm not the poster child for clean living."

Kelsey frowned. "What's that supposed to mean? You haven't fallen into a bad crowd since moving here, have you, Ry?"

I had to laugh. "Is there even such a thing in Crescent Cove?"

"Of course there is. This a small town, but there's still a criminal element and shady characters."

"Where? I've never seen one. And I gotta say, you sound so adorably prim and proper right now. This kid is going to be very well-mannered or else lose his mind and join a rock band." I patted her beach ball belly as she gasped.

"A rock band? Those heathens?" But she was grinning, which I suspected was as much for my benefit as out of real amusement.

Forget her reaction to her kid being in a rock band. I'd prefer to see Dare's. He'd probably ground him for life—even after he was of age. Dungeon, anyone?

"You don't have to worry. I'm not doing anything dangerous. I definitely couldn't now, even if I wanted to."

"What's that supposed to mean?"

"Today is supposed to be about you and your little dude. Not me and my...issues." Though saying it that way felt wrong. My kid might be scaring the holy hell out of me, but he or she wasn't a problem. I refused to see my baby that way. The last thing I wanted to do was traumatize the child before he or she was even born.

Besides, Gage seemed totally on-board with the idea. So weird. Why wasn't he having panic attacks like most men who knocked up a random stranger would be? We were family, sort of, but that was an accident of...well, procreation too when it came right down to it. Who knew if Kelsey and Dare would've gotten married if she hadn't been pregnant? I mean, they were completely gonzo over each other—anyone could see that—but the baby had certainly pushed them together.

Just like you and Gage.

Hmm. Yeah, no. Not the same at all. Gage wouldn't be proposing anytime soon.

I didn't think.

Would he?

I fought back a shiver and looked up at my sister, who was staring at me. "Rylee, you better spill. Pronto."

"You should sit down."

"That good, huh?" But she followed my directive and eased herself into the chair beside me.

I fiddled with the donkey's tail on the salt-shaker. "You can't tell Mom or Dad yet. I will. Soon. Probably soon."

Kelsey just waited.

"So, it turns out I'm a little bit pregnant."

Kelsey's red eyebrows climbed toward her hairline. "Come again?"

"I'm knocked up. Like you. Well, not like you. Holy ready to burst." I shuddered. "But you know, same concept."

On the bright side, my sister did not look at me as if I'd grown another set of eyeballs or something equally horrific. She also did not cheer with unabashed joy.

Not really surprising about the joy part, considering I was

unemployed and technically single and unemployed and technically single.

Yes, both bore repeating.

"Are you sure?"

A telltale tickle made me clear my throat. "According to Clear Blue Easy, Oopsy Daisy You're Expecting, and Momma Beans, yes, I am."

"Rylee." Kelsey pressed her hands to her cheeks. "I—I don't know what to say."

That my normally chatty sister didn't even have a comment made my eyes ache. They didn't fill again, thank God, just burned. "That makes two of us."

"Are you..." She stopped and took a breath. "This wasn't planned?"

That I could still laugh was a minor miracle. "No. Definitely not."

"Are you keeping it?"

I nodded vehemently. On that one point, I was certain. "Yes. This is my baby."

Even as I said the words aloud, I heard Gage correcting me in my head.

Our baby.

"And the father?" Kelsey laced her fingers together over her swollen belly. "Have you thought of how you're going to tell him?"

"Don't have to. He was there when I found out."

"Oh."

Yep, that was my sister, being all loquacious. "Oh?" I repeated.

"Yes, that's a good sign then, if he's involved that much. How did he react?"

"He kept me from hitting the floor. So, I'd say that's a plus." I rubbed my forehead. "Look, this is a tricky situation for all of us, but I wanted to give you a head's up so you had time to get used to the idea before Dare finds out and gets all...Dare."

"Why would Dare have an opinion? He's your brother-in-law and he cares about you of course, but he wouldn't presume to overstep and offer opinions where they weren't wanted."

"Because um, hello, the father is Gage. You really think Dare won't insert his size thirteens and get all up in our business?"

I'd never seen a person pale before my eyes. Especially considering my sister was practically Casper the friendly ghost's cousin in terms of skin tone to begin with. But yep, it was really a thing.

I was getting all kinds of educations this week. Lucky me.

"Whoops, sorry, I'm guessing you didn't make that connection." I looked down at my mostly flat belly and sighed. "Just call us two sisters for two brothers, Kel, because you aren't the only Ford to get knocked up by a Kramer."

"Oh, God." Kelsey buried her face in her hands, her long red ponytail flopping forward over her head like a droopy penis. Lord, I had sex on the brain. "Oh, God."

"That good, huh?"

"Dare is going to flip. He's already got issues with Gage, and if he finds out he was irresponsible enough to knock you up, along with quitting racing—"

"Hold up, sister. What do you mean that he was irresponsible enough to knock me up when it takes two to tango? Also, uh, didn't Dare plant his flag in your fertile bush before the bonds of matrimony had taken place?"

Just like that, color flooded Kelsey's cheeks to replace all that she'd lost. "That was different."

"Why, because now you're happily married so the past doesn't count?"

"Never mind that. Are you sure it's Gage's? Maybe it's not. Maybe it's someone else's."

"Excuse me? Do you think I'm some sort of hussy?" Indignation had me grabbing the donkey salt-shaker and waving it for emphasis. After I made sure the little holes were closed.

See, I could be practical.

"No, of course not. It's just sometimes hard to be certain. When I found out I was pregnant, I wasn't sure who the father was at first, and it didn't make me a hussy." Kel frowned. "Though it was my one and only chance to say I was one, so maybe I should own it?"

"You own what you like. And seriously? You let Tommy slip you the sausage while you were riding Dare's pony?"

"Too many metaphors. Save my brain."

My lips twitched despite the situation. "After you had coitus with Dare, you really went back and had intercourse with Tommy? How?"

"Other way around, and it wasn't that cut and dried. Tommy was just a one-time thing after his grandma's funeral, and Dare brought me a pizza and—" She flushed up to her hairline and waved it off. "Anyway, this baby is Dare's and we're talking about you. I just wanted to make sure you had the DNA right. No shame in it if you've been with another guy."

"Oh, the DNA's right. No doubt there. I haven't been with anyone else but him in all these months." I set down the donkey and sighed. "Haven't wanted to be either. He broke me somehow. And going back for seconds didn't make me lose interest either. He's got a magic tongue and magic hands and a magic—"

"Stop. Brother-in-law. Don't make it weird when he passes the gravy boat, please."

I had to laugh as I rubbed my thumbs under my eyes. I hated crying. "While we're on the subject, do you mind giving me the name of your doctor here? I'd planned on just going back to Turnbull, but it seems like I'll be at the doc's more often for a bit. Local would be handier."

Also, when it came time to give birth, closer was better. Since I would be in unrelenting agony and all, considering pumpkins weren't supposed to be shoved out of narrow places. No matter what my biology teacher had said.

Yeah, I wasn't going to think about that part yet.

"Sure. My doctor is fabulous. You'll love her. The info is in my planner."

"Of course. My super organized sister."

And me? I thought I was doing well if I managed to remember what TV shows I wanted to DVR.

"I know it makes it awkward for you."

"Forget me. Dare is going to have a kitten. He already thinks Gage can't even remember to mail an envelope, and now he's going to be responsible for a kid?" Kelsey's frown lines deepened about six inches. "He is taking responsibility, isn't he?"

"Well, it's early days yet, but he seems to be. He's been very attentive. Almost too much."

"Kramer family trait." Kelsey nodded sagely. "But we'll make sure he understands this is an eighteen-year commitment. Just so he doesn't think he can dabble."

Before I could ask what exactly that whole *we* thing meant, the front door opened with a wave of female laughter.

My belly clenched and I was pretty sure it wasn't just because I was already ready for dinner though it was barely past lunch.

Kelsey squeezed my hand and lurched to her feet. "In here, girls."

Sage Hamilton and Ally Hamilton strolled in, laden with bags of party gear. They stopped dead at the sight of me, though both quickly smiled. "Rylee. How nice to see you. Are you coming shopping with us?"

I smiled weakly at Ally. "Yeah, I figured I'd see what all went down at Baby Rama."

God help me.

"Just as well you learn now before—" Kel broke off and clapped as she smiled brightly. "So, whatcha got in the bags?"

I didn't cover my face, but it was close. My sister was legendary for opening her mouth and inserting hands, feet, and half her torso.

Lucky me.

Ally cleared her throat and glanced between me and my sister with obvious empathy. "Stuff for the shower. It was touch and go collecting it all from Sage and Oliver's due to the projectile vomiting."

I shrank back in horror. "Oliver?"

Sage's eyebrows beetled. "Do you know my husband? He would need to be tranquilized before he endured such natural bodily functions. No, Star. My poor baby." She sighed. "Stupid virus. I hated leaving her."

"She's with Seth and Oliver," Ally said with a soothing arm pat.

"I hated leaving her," Sage repeated. "Those two with two babies and Laurie? God."

"Seth has raised a child of his own through babyhood and into first grade. I'm quite certain he can handle Star's little spot of the flu."

"She was erupting from both ends."

I was looking under the table, trying to see if I could fit under it, when my sister tugged on my braid. "Don't scare Ry senseless."

"Star's fine." Ally waved it off. "You don't know my best friend very well, Rylee, but she has a flair for the dramatic. Oliver barely blinked when we left."

"If barely blinked means he was practically on his knees, begging me not to leave." Sage pulled out a kitchen chair and set down her pile of bags, half of which toppled over and hit the floor.

Though Kelsey was as big as the circular table, she immediately tried to bend over to clean up the mess. Sage, however, was too busy gesturing with her hands to notice.

"Tip for you, Ry, since you're the youngest of us. Men are basically children, no matter how old they are. They pretend to be so competent, and they can handle things like hammering nails and such, but when it comes to the biggies? Like changing diapers and staying up with sick babies and wiping up diarrhea off child seats? Yeah, they suck."

Ally hurried forward to help Kelsey. "Don't paw through those. That's shower stuff. You can't see the theme until the big day."

Kelsey beamed. "Aww, I love circus animals. That's so sweet."

Too late there.

"I told you we should've left this stuff at your place," Ally said over her shoulder to Sage. "Now the surprise is ruined."

"My house needs a full Lysol sweep. I didn't want to risk infecting Kel. Do you know how potent that virus is?"

"So, you bring your child over to spend the day with mine? Thanks, bestie." Ally flipped Sage the middle finger.

Had I really been mildly jealous of my sister being tight with these women? It must be pregnancy hormones. They were very chatty and shared far too much about bodily functions.

Macy's snark and lack of interest in anything baby-related was much more my speed.

Welcome to your new reality, baby girl. Your world is going to be full of kid stuff.

"Really, you both could've skipped today. Ry is here. She can help me set up the registry—"

"Oh, come on, Oliver and Seth are in each other's pockets constantly. Star will be infecting Alex any day now. Maybe this way he'll build up some immunity."

"Or maybe Seth and Oliver will both get sick and we'll be in hell." Ally shook Sage's shoulders. "*Hell,* woman."

"Is this what it's like being knocked up by brothers?" I wondered aloud, causing everyone to turn my way.

I realized after the fact that my question sounded much different than my intent.

"Um, I don't mean one woman being knocked up by brothers. I mean, like if you and your sister—" I cleared my throat. Yes, Kelsey and I were definitely biologically related, judging by our mouths. "It was on *Jerry* yesterday. Good episode."

"Oh, wow, you're still with Dare's brother? Holy shit. I thought that was just a one-nighter deal. Judging from the wedding fireworks —" Sage broke off and nudged Ally out of the way to come over to the table. "He's delicious. Go you."

"Uh, thanks? And no, we aren't really together in that sense." I bit my lip. "Sometimes it's just sex and you get pregnant."

Even as I said the words, they didn't seem quite right. Sure, that night in December, we'd been riding the lust train. But now? We weren't exactly out of that place, but it seemed like we were kind of straddling another one too. Friends with benefits, maybe, but more? Or it could be more, if I wasn't a freak who was too scared to let the guy spend the night.

Or the afternoon.

Sage looked around the room at the other women. "Hello, you're preaching to the choir. We all were in that situation. Well, minus Ally because she was in love with Seth since the moment he insulted her in like, what was it, seventh grade?"

"Tenth. And it wasn't an insult. Exactly." Ally whacked Sage lightly on the arm. "What my big-mouthed bestie means is sometimes an accident can lead to…well, a miracle."

Sage frowned. "I didn't mean that, but that's really sweet."

I looked down at the table. My hands were fisted, the knuckles white. I wasn't used to miracles. My life was mostly a train wreck collision most of the time, broken up by stretches of boredom that caused me to do something crazy.

Like climbing Gage like a stripper pole that night at The Spinning Wheel.

"I don't know what this is yet," I said, hating that everyone was looking at me.

Waiting for me to declare that I was madly in love with Gage.

Or that he was madly in love with me.

It didn't always work out that way. I didn't want to borrow trouble and expect something that might not be in the cards. My priority was my kid.

Our kid.

Gage and I were incidental to making sure the baby got what he or she needed. If we managed to figure that out, I wouldn't ask for more.

No matter how much part of me wanted to.

THIRTEEN

Babies needed a lot of stuff.

For someone who was newly unemployed—again—Baby Rama was overwhelming. Forget even the cost of things. The sheer amount of items needed to properly provide for a child was staggering.

How did people manage?

The kid would need pacifiers and special cups that didn't spill, and head supports and pillows to brace their floppy frames. Toys. Clothes.

A place to live.

Was my apartment big enough for us? It didn't seem so, since it was scarcely big enough for me. I could dance in the living room and almost touch all four walls.

I had savings, thank God, and I suspected Gage wouldn't skimp on helping out, but he'd probably be hitting the road soon. He'd indicated he wasn't thinking about racing right now, but everyone needed a break sometimes. No matter what he'd said, he'd probably just temporarily hit the pause button on his life. It was in his blood too much for him to not go back.

Wasn't it?

We'd have to work out visitation schedules and child support and so many other things.

At least not today.

Lord, there were so many kinds of diapers. How was a person supposed to know which to pick? I didn't even know if I was having a girl or boy yet, but they had certain patterns for wetness and diapers suited for each.

The world of parenting was a vast, terrifying place, and I had no handbook.

While my sister and her girl crew were squealing over tiny shoes and sandals, I leaped upon my version of the Holy Grail—*What to Expect When You're Expecting.*

There was even a sign for it, right in the middle of a rack of many other frightening baby books.

That would be my savior. An easy, step by step guide that hopefully didn't have too much scary terminology.

Some people were frightened of clowns or horror movies. Not me. I could watch just about anything with Macy without even hiding my eyes.

But sweet mercy, I still hadn't recovered from hearing about something called a "mucus plug" from my cheerfully informative sister. Somehow she'd developed a feeling of Zen toward the birthing process.

I had not reached that place yet.

I might not ever get there, especially if I couldn't find this fucking book.

"Where is it?" Sweat blurred into my eyes as I dug through the other books, tossing them to and fro, desperate to find one copy. I needed the latest version, in case there were new discoveries or something.

I wasn't going to start my parenting adventure with an outdated copy. Maybe one before they even knew mucus plugs existed.

On the other hand, perhaps that wouldn't be so bad.

"There has to be one left. Just one." I spun around and came face to face with Kelsey. Or face to breasts, because my sister was taller than me and her boobs were fairly ginormous right now.

"What's wrong with you? You're all sweaty and pale." She held a hand to my forehead. "You feel hot. Oh jeez, I hope you don't have that same virus little Star does."

"Star sounds like a hooker's name," I snapped, backing up to get some air.

And bumped right into the little swiveling rack of books. They all went flying, and look at that, there was my book.

I dove on it like a seagull swarming toward the last French fry, clutching it to my chest and throwing out a hand to ward off the approaching blue-clad Baby Rama worker. I knew she worked there because they had these dopey little hats that looked like beanies with propellers.

If it was supposed to be cute, it failed. Miserably.

"Mine," I enunciated carefully, fully ready to do battle if she tried to pry it out of my hands.

I didn't know why she would, just that I'd caused a scene and made a mess and oh yeah, called Sage's baby a hooker. At least I had to assume that was why the normally friendly blond was staring at me with a murderous expression.

Oops.

"I didn't mean she was a hooker, or even would be one, because she's a baby. Just that her name is very—well, sexualized. Or it could be, if you watch too many movies." I crossed my arms over my chest and swallowed a whimper as she came toward me. I wasn't a street fighter, and this woman clearly had the rage advantage. "Personally, I love the name."

Before she reached me, I booked down the aisle, hopping over the couple of books that had somehow been flung farther than the others. I needed to clean up my disaster, but first, I needed to flee. I had a child to protect.

Good story, Ry.

Two aisles over, my sister caught up with me. She was huffing and puffing, which made me feel momentarily guilty until she spoke.

"You need to apologize to Sage."

I winced. "Didn't I already do that?" Kinda.

"That was very mean what you said."

"I didn't mean to lash out at her. I'm just a little freaked out right now. Look at this place." I waved my hand at the rows of car seats and strollers and a million different contraptions I didn't even have a clue what to do with. "It's crazy. How can a newborn need this many things? How do people not go into the poorhouse? Oh, I know, land yourself a richy rich Hamilton—"

Kelsey's hand covered my mouth. Probably wisely. "You have insulted my friends enough for one day. And besides, a little hypocritical, aren't you? Gage isn't exactly a pauper."

She dropped her hand and I tipped back my head to take a deep breath. "You're right. I'm going crazy."

At least I didn't immediately launch into all the reasons Gage's wealth had nothing to do with me providing for my child. I was progressing.

Not that anyone would be able to tell from the last few minutes.

This was like the situation with Kathy, except worse, because Sage hadn't done anything to harm me. She hadn't even given me attitude. She was just so blond and pretty and self-assured, with her perfect husband and adorable vomiting hooker-baby.

Bad Rylee.

"I'm not assuming anything there."

"Because he's irresponsible," Kelsey said flatly, crossing her arms. "You're steeling yourself against certain disappointment."

"No, I didn't say that."

Well, maybe a little.

"I'm your sister. You can be honest with me about your fears. I'm on your side."

The compassion in her expression nearly undid me. Instead, I held up the book I'd fought wars for. "This is going to tell me how to do everything. I won't feel so helpless and stupid after I read this."

Kelsey sighed. "It's just a book, Ry. Not a fairy godmother who will grant you all the knowledge in the universe." She rubbed the side of her belly. "Maybe you should talk to Mom?"

"Why?"

"She raised two girls. Might have some insight, you know."

"Well, yeah, I'm sure she does. But what is she going to say when she hears I'm knocked up too, just like you were?"

"I'm sure she'll be shocked and appalled, but she'll probably recover. Someday. After lots of therapy."

I paced away from her up the aisle and picked up a giraffe that lit up and giggled maniacally. Creepy. I set it back down. "I'm not like you, Kel. She knows I can't hold a job. I'm not a stable teacher with a planner that has my life detailed out to the nth degree. I'm lucky if I can remember to buy TP."

"Yet I still had to deal with an unexpected situation," she reminded me. "Life happens."

Sometimes I hated how reasonable my sister was. It was probably why she'd been born first. If I'd been the older sister, my advice would've been stuff like, "Never combine beer with hard liquor."

"You had Dare though. He knew how to do the kid thing. Gage is as clueless as I am."

"And he's not exactly the kind of man to step up and offer his hand either."

I frowned. "Hand for what?"

She moved closer and extended her arms to place her hands on my shoulders. With her rapidly increased belly size, she couldn't quite hug me the way she once had.

That would be me soon enough. Especially due to my peanut butter obsession.

"I know it's scary to be going through this alone. But I'm here for you. Dare and I both will be, if you need anything. Like…a loan or a place to stay—"

"I told you, I'm not alone. He's trying." Why couldn't she believe that? Were Kel and Dare that determined to believe the worst about Gage?

I could get why I was seen as the Ford family fuck-up. But Gage was a millionaire. Had to be. He'd been super successful in his career and could do anything he wanted. Yet they acted as if he couldn't be trusted to put down the toilet seat.

"I understand that you want to hope for the best."

"Of course I do, but it's not Gage I'm worried about." Or not entirely. Pretty much everything had me panicked at the moment. "I just don't know what the future is going to look like. I'm not the girl who needs to plan out every day in advance, but it feels like I have to now. Because I don't want to screw up this baby. It just feels like I'm destined to."

"Can you give us a second?"

I went still at the perky voice coming from behind us. Mainly because I felt like it was a trap. Sage shouldn't be sounding that way toward me after my heinous remark.

Kel apparently thought the same because her hands tightened on my shoulders. "I was going to take her over to Baby Rama Eats. She should keep up her strength."

"Oh, I'm starving. I'll buy her some French fries." Sage reached for my hand and tugged me with her.

Helplessly, I waved at my sister. I nearly mouthed, "call 911," but I managed not to.

There was a small restaurant attached to the baby store. Tacking on the equivalent of a McDonald's complete with play area onto a kid shop was a little odd, but I supposed it was an ingenious way to keep the children busy and fed while the parents shopped.

Sage was true to her word and bought us both French fries and milkshakes. Vanilla for me, chocolate for her. We sat at a tiny table shaped like a mushroom and I ate rapidly while I tried not to make it obvious that I was half waiting for Sage to pull out a weapon from her boat-sized purse.

"I'm not mad at you," Sage announced.

"I'm sorry I said that. I'm not myself right now."

Sadly, I was very much myself. I said rude things that got me in trouble often. I just had the excuse of pregnancy hormones along with exhaustion and worries I couldn't discuss with my sister.

She probably didn't even remember I turned into a zombie sometimes after dark. She was already concerned enough that Gage and I were completely incapable of raising an infant that I wasn't about to remind her of my issue as a teenager.

As a teenager *and* currently. Yay me.

Sage shrugged. "Actually, my husband would probably agree with you. Which I will admit is part of the reason I insisted that we named her Star. Oliver needed some shaking up. If it'd been up to him, he would've probably named her Eleanor Mildred."

I snorted and inhaled salt off my fry into a place it should not go. Once I'd soothed my throat with some of my shake, I had to grin. "He does seem a little uptight."

"Most of the time." The way she said it made me think that Oliver was capable of shedding his prim and proper attitude when necessary, but we weren't close enough for me to pump her for salacious information.

"She really is a gorgeous baby. I'm probably just jealous." Saying it aloud was a revelation.

Because I probably was.

I'd never thought I wanted a kid or a husband. At least not yet. But now that I was pregnant, I was suddenly aware of all I didn't have. My life felt so tenuous. For the first time, security was the most appealing thing in the world.

Was this my version of nesting? I'd thought that happened in like the eighth month or something.

I sneaked a glance at the purchased book now tucked securely in the plastic bag at my hip. I'd find out all the details about how pregnancy worked soon enough.

God help me.

"Thanks." Sage unwrapped her straw. "We're more alike than you realize."

"We are?"

"Yes. I realize we barely know each other, but I've gotten the feeling from Kel you weren't the settling down type."

"Accurate."

Partly for reasons people couldn't begin to guess. I didn't know how to trust a guy. And if I couldn't trust a dude with a sleep disorder millions of people dealt with, why bother trying to build a relationship beyond the physical?

I knew not all men were dicks. Some would understand. It was just that risking it felt so huge and scary, and I'd never met anyone since Shane who seemed worth the leap.

Until now. Maybe.

"I had always told myself I wanted to have a husband and kids, but not yet. I was a virgin, for God's sake. I wanted to play the field a little. At least get *on* the field, you know?" She slurped hard on her straw.

"Yeah, I do." I played with my straw wrapper. "It's different for guys."

"So different. But once I came to terms with being pregnant, I realized I didn't really want to play the field, because I'd already found more than I'd hoped for. If you strike gold, why go back to mining for iron?"

"Well, iron isn't exactly a bad thing to find, but yeah."

"You know what I mean. I'm just saying maybe look on the bright side. You're panicking and overwhelmed, understandably, but Gage is right there with you. Or he should be."

"He is," I said quietly.

So far, he'd been more supportive than I could've ever asked for. Family or not, we were basically strangers who liked to see each other without our clothes.

"That said, I'm having extreme mommy guilt about leaving my hooker baby when she's sick."

It took me a minute to hear what Sage had said, but once I did, a laugh spilled out before I could stop it. I covered my mouth with my hand. "Oh, God, I'm really sorry. Please forgive me?"

She grinned and popped a fry in her mouth. "Don't worry about it. But I'm about to ask you for a favor."

"Sure. I basically owe you anything you could possibly ask for."

"Would you help Kel and Ally go through the store and find stuff for the registry? I hate to bail, but I really need to be home. And not even because Oliver can't manage to take care of the baby, because he's frighteningly competent at most things. I just miss her. I want to be the one who cares for her. With him." Sage's cheeks bloomed pink and I ducked my head, more embarrassed than if she'd started talking about her sex life.

Seeing someone so in love with her kid and her husband was even more intimate.

And I wanted that. I wanted to be the woman who couldn't wait to get home to my child and my guy, even if they were puking.

Well, the kid. I'd probably rather not deal with a sick man, ever, since they were worse than any infant. When my dad was sick, my mom usually wanted to hide in the basement with a pint of Ben and Jerry's.

Or a jug of wine.

"Go ahead. I'll do registry detail. Sister bonding activity and all that. Besides, we're all moms here. We get it."

Holy crap. I was a mom.

Or almost a mom, though probably being an incubator counted.

"Thanks. You're the best. Though you may get a call from my husband when I slip and refer to Star as the hooker baby." She grinned and waved, grabbing our tray—with my half-eaten French fries, but whatever—on her way out.

I saw her chatting with and then hugging Ally and Kel inside the store before she split. Not ten minutes later, a sleek black sports car showed up at the curb and she slipped inside. I looked away but looked back again when the car lingered. They were clearly engaged in a marathon kiss. Which was a positive sign that romance didn't die after childbirth.

Then again, I hadn't had any romance yet. So, what was I worried about?

I chewed on my straw.

Everything.

I was worried about everything.

When I rejoined Ally and Kel, they'd filled the cart with all kinds of baby goodness. Scary stuff like industrial containers of wipes—for industrial amounts of poop—and truly small onesies. I wanted to go back to check out the books again, but I didn't want to return to the scene of the crime quite so soon. Besides, it was time to pick out the stuff Kel wanted her guests to get her as presents for the shower.

Dutifully, I scanned the items she wanted, listening to endless debates about the merits of certain car seats and swings and baby bathtubs. That one vexed me. I mean, why couldn't the kid be washed in a regular tub?

"It's too large. The baby needs to feel secure."

I stared at Kel. "I don't think Mom washed me in any special bathtub."

"Yes, and see how you turned out?"

I didn't have an argument for that one. But I also wasn't putting any fancy schmancy plastic deal on my registry either.

If I needed one.

If anyone even bothered to give me a shower.

My closest friend in town was Macy, and she wasn't exactly one to plan games of the pin the rattle on the baby donkey variety. So, that left my sister.

"Not that we're keeping track or anything, but you'll do this for me, right?"

"Hmm?" Kel picked up a package of baby-sized plastic feeding dishes and carefully studied the back.

They even had to have their own plates, for pity's sake. They were like a strange little alien subset of humanity.

Perhaps I was more like Macy than I'd realized.

"I don't really have any friends." I swallowed hard as my sister gave me a sidelong glance. "I have a couple back home, and Macy is kind of becoming a friend, but she's sort of anti-baby and I don't know anyone who'd give me a shower. The baby will need all kinds of stuff and I'm okay with going without, but I don't really want him or her to."

"Oh, sweetie, of course I'll give you a shower." Kel dropped the package in her cart and turned to cup my cheeks. "It's not every day my baby sister has her first baby."

"First and possibly last, depending how badly I screw this one up."

"That's the spirit. Positive thinking for the win." She shook her head. "Seriously, Ry, you're just in that initial panic stage. Sooner rather than later, you'll relax."

"I don't think so. I'm pretty sure I won't relax for the next eighteen years."

"Well, that may be true, but—" She grew silent as Ally came careening around the other end of the aisle, her brows knitted together and her eyes wild. "What's wrong?" Kel asked.

"Sage went to collect Star, but not fast enough. Now Alex is throwing up and he just splashed Laurie and she's screaming like he tried to murder her. Seth is at his wit's end. I have to go too. I'm so sorry."

"Oh, no. That's okay. We're basically done. You've already helped so much."

"Yeah, but I just remembered I drove us all here. I can drop you off on the way—"

Kelsey shook her head. "No worries. I'll call Dare. He'll be getting off work soon anyway. Go on, go home to your family."

"If you're sure. Thanks, Kel. Congratulations to you, Rylee." Ally smiled. "Exciting times."

"Thank you."

It was only after Ally left that I realized she was the first person who'd congratulated me on being pregnant. As if it was a good thing rather than the scourge of the earth.

"Let me just call Dare—"

"Wait, I can call Gage—"

Too late.

Kel was on the phone with my brother-in-law, and that meant the chances of Kel spilling the baby beans before we arrived home were high. Either way, Dare would know by tonight that his brother was the irresponsible inseminator, but I'd prefer not to be there when the information was shared.

Asking Kel to keep a lid on it was pretty much useless. She would try. It was just her lips were about as secure as a child's lunchbox.

Jeez, I was already thinking in kid terms. Children didn't even have lunch boxes anymore, did they? Paper sacks or lunch lines were where it was at.

Along with getting pregnant, I'd plunged back into *Little House on the Prairie* times in my own head.

"He'll be on his way in a few," Kel said to me.

I tried to smile. Yay.

Once Kel got off the phone, we checked out her massive cart of stuff. We'd just made it outside when Kel's very safe sedan slid up to the curb. The trunk lid lifted just before Dare climbed out. He took a look at Kelsey's pile of purchases, then hurried over to help us load it all into the car.

"We havin' twins and I missed it?" There was no missing the rumble in his voice—or the hard kiss he gave my sister before she had a chance to answer.

Romance was all around me. It took all shapes and forms, but it was there.

The passenger door opened, and I blinked as Gage unfolded himself from the front seat. Somehow I'd missed him in my observation of my brother-in-law and my sister.

All of a sudden, I couldn't stop watching how couples interacted. As if this was a subject I needed to dissect and master.

"Hey." He didn't so much as glance at the other two before striding over to me and planting one on me.

Not on my forehead.

Not a chaste little peck hello.

Oh, no, Gage brought it all the way home with soft, warm lips, a hint of tongue, and a low groan that made my nipples harden and my panties soak.

So, maybe I didn't need romance. Maybe I'd just settle for another hard fuck. Hey, look at that pretty wrought iron park bench over there—

"What're you saying about park benches?" He pulled back enough to laugh at me.

I pressed my forehead to his chest. "Just pondering you fucking me on one. Don't pay me any mind."

"Oh, I'll definitely pay that some mind." He trailed his fingers down the side of my face and tipped up my chin. "Baby shopping, huh?"

But he didn't look at the big hulking store behind us. He kept his gaze on mine.

"For my sister."

His thumb swept along my lower lip. He didn't say anything, just kept rubbing and devouring me with his eyes.

And I liked it.

A lot.

"You two going to get a move on anytime soon?" Dare didn't give us time to answer before he turned his back on us to open Kelsey's car door.

Kelsey sent me an apologetic glance before shifting toward Gage. Her expression in his direction wasn't nearly so friendly. "She's probably tired. The first tri—" She licked her lips and darted a glance at Dare. "So, rough day at work?"

"Never mind that. What were you going to say?"

"You told her," Gage said in an undertone while Kelsey stalled by playing with her maternity top.

I nodded. "She's my sister."

"You might as well just get it out in the open," I said to her. "You know you'll tell him before the night is through anyway."

At least he'd have to say his rude comments to us instead of behind our backs.

"It's your news to tell." Kelsey pressed her lips together and slipped into the car.

"Dare, I'm pregnant. And your brother is the father."

It was easier to say the words this time. Maybe by the time I reached my parents, it'd be as easy as talking about the weather. Assuming the grapevine didn't reach them first.

Dare shut Kelsey's door and shifted to face us, crossing his arms. But his focus was all for his brother. "So, you decided to take single parenthood for a spin?"

Gage reached down and took my hand, and I was grateful for the united front. Though I wouldn't have minded hitching a ride home rather than getting in that car with our older siblings.

I felt very much like the high school kid who'd been caught climbing in a window past curfew, and I didn't appreciate it one bit. From Gage's tight jaw, he didn't either.

"Does this look single to you?" Gage lifted our joined hands. "Looks like we're in this together."

"For now." Dare shook his head and circled the car to get in behind the wheel. His slamming of his car door made me wince.

"He has no right," Gage muttered. "I'm not a fucking child."

"No, and neither am I. But no one thinks we can do this." I tried to swallow past the lump in my throat. "Maybe we can't."

FOURTEEN

I COULDN'T BELIEVE WHAT I WAS HEARING.

Dare giving me attitude was nothing new. In fact, I'd expected it.

Same with Rylee's sister. She'd married my brother, hadn't she? So, it wasn't a stretch to think she'd see things the way Dare did.

But for Rylee to join in with them? It felt like a betrayal.

I knew she was scared. This was all so new to her. Hell, I was too. But what she'd said sounded dangerously like giving up. And Christ, we'd barely gotten started.

"No one gets a manual on how to have kids. Not even Oscar over there. He had to figure it out as he went along just like everyone else does." I squeezed Rylee's suddenly cold hand. "Just like we will."

She didn't get to reply before Kelsey rolled down her window. "Dare has to get back to the shop, guys."

Even that held a note of reprisal.

Stop screwing around, kids, and get in the car.

"We could get an Uber," I said to Rylee.

She tugged on my hand. "The car is already here. Besides, does Crescent Cove even have Uber? I'd think it would have to come from Syracuse and that would be forty-five minutes. And sorry, I have to pee."

I didn't remind her the store she'd just come from had to have a bathroom, since some women were touchy about public restrooms. Whatever. It wasn't that long a ride. And Dare would probably temper his reactions due to witnesses.

Not that I gave a shit what he had to say. He was my older brother, and I'd always looked up to the guy, but I didn't need any more grief about how I was living my life. I was doing my best. It wasn't as if I'd screwed up yet, for fuck's sake.

Minus knocking up Rylee in the first place, but stuff happened.

We got in the back of Kelsey's sedan. The silence lasted approximately until the first turn out of the parking lot.

"So, you going to let Mom and Dad know about the blessed event any time soon? Since I was just there and Dad sure didn't mention you needing a car seat for your pussy mobile."

"Nah, I figured I'd wait till Rylee popped and bring the kid to Thanksgiving instead of cranberry sauce. Surprise!"

Rylee was not amused by my comment. She punched me hard in the thigh and then tucked her hands under her arms.

United front? Okay then.

"It just happened," Kelsey said in a low tone to Dare, clearly trying to calm him down.

Though why he was so agitated, I had no idea. He himself had knocked up Kelsey long before their marriage ceremony—hell, even before they were dating. As I recalled overhearing, he'd delivered her a pizza, with a side of dick. Who was he to act so high and mighty?

"Really? Though they interrupted our wedding with their shenanigans? I find that highly unlikely."

My brother used to not speak. Now he was using words like "shenanigans." I blamed Kelsey for this new and unwelcome change.

"She doesn't mean 'it' just happened," Rylee said. "She means we just found out."

"What are your plans?" Dare asked as if his wife and her sister had never spoken.

I started to reply, but Rylee cut me off. Probably a good thing, because I'd been about to say some shit that most likely would've gotten me banned at the family dinner table for the foreseeable future.

"We're still figuring stuff out. It's all so new."

"You're going to have a child in that closet-sized apartment?"

"No, I'd planned on having it in a hospital. I'm not some earth mother type."

Even I had to laugh at that one.

Kelsey cleared her throat. "He means it's kind of a small place, Ry. But you don't have to figure all that out just yet. The gestation period gives you some time."

"Not that much time. If she's going to need a new lease, rentals are full up in Crescent Cove, especially during the summer. She'll want to start looking now."

"Yeah, as soon as we get the kid's college choice locked down, we'll move right on to that. Chop, chop."

No one responded to me. Not even Rylee.

Hey, what did my opinion on the subject matter? I was just the sperm donor.

"You're actually probably right." Rylee fiddled with the handle of the shopping bag I hadn't noticed until right now. "I'll have to make a budget and see what's available. Of course I need a job. Money would help."

"I'll see if I can find out more about that receptionist position. That would be great for you, Ry."

I frowned. "At the school?"

Kelsey nodded. "Yes, ours suddenly quit."

Dare grunted his hard-won approval. "That'd be a good place to get in. Solid benefits and vacation time. Summers off."

"She doesn't need to work if she doesn't want to. I have enough money if she wants to stay home and—"

"Excuse me, stay home? We haven't discussed this. And while I appreciate you offering support to our child, I don't need to be a kept woman."

"We haven't discussed it because it just happened." With effort, I relaxed my jaw. "I'm not saying you have to stay home, just that it's an option. It would make it easier for—"

"For who, you? When you're off racing cars and leaving all the child-rearing to my sister?" Kelsey crossed her arms in a mirror of her sister's pose.

"I'm done racing."

"For now," Dare added ominously as he braked for a light as slowly as a great-grandmother.

I said nothing. Why bother? If I'd said Rylee should get three jobs to support herself, I would've been labeled a thoughtless jerk. If I said I'd gladly support her, I was equally bad. I couldn't win.

And she hadn't even mentioned this receptionist's position to me. So, yeah, what did my thoughts have to do with anything? Evidently, not much.

"We aren't like you guys," Rylee said after a moment, her voice surprisingly soft. "Dare knew what having a kid was like, and we're really inexperienced. But we have good role models to watch and learn from."

Kelsey shifted in her seat and gave Rylee a smile. "You'll be just fine. It's a learning curve for everyone. That book should help."

Before I could ask, Rylee pushed the bag she'd brought with her into my lap. I pulled out the book and flipped through the pages while Kelsey and Rylee chatted about innocuous things like school assemblies and Kelsey's upcoming baby shower.

Dare offered his usual grunts.

I had the misfortune of landing on the chapter that talked about some issues impending moms could have while pregnant. Cervical insufficiency and high blood pressure and hemorrhoids and excessive bloating among them.

Dear Lord, why did anyone inflict this on themselves intentionally? Not that we had, but people tried to have kids every day.

The changes a pregnant woman went through were insane. Bumpy areolas? Sensitive nipples? Which sounded okay from my end but not the way it was described. The aforementioned hemorrhoids and bloating, along with nausea and Rylee's exhaustion. And that was if the pregnancy went well. If it didn't, there could be complications and those were far worse.

"Are your nipples sore?"

I hadn't meant to blurt that out—especially in mixed company—but this book was seriously messing with my head.

Rylee frowned. "Like right now?"

"Jesus, man." Dare shook his head. "Seriously?"

Kelsey glanced back at me with one eyebrow raised. "You need to ease in with that book. Maybe read a chapter a day or something. It can be overwhelming."

"I was on the first chapter. It's terrifying."

"Why?" Rylee scooted closer to me on the seat, and only then did I realize she wasn't belted in. "What page are you on?"

"You need to be safe." I shifted her back and leaned over her to grab her belt, notching it securely around her.

"Aww, that's sweet." Kelsey sounded pleased, but Rylee's expression held no similar joy.

"Give me that book, Gage."

I was already back skimming the page I'd been on. "Sometimes there's leaking. I mean, what? Are you planning on breastfeeding?"

"Is this really necessary right now?" My brother sounded strangled.

I couldn't blame him. I felt the same.

I'd been so calm and collected about this whole baby situation. Sure, I'd had my own private moments of flipping out. But ignorance was surely bliss, because holy shit, I'd had no clue of what this would actually entail.

Forget the whole eighteen years thing. Just the process of getting the baby out of her sounded like a horror show.

"This is why men don't endure childbirth." Kelsey surprised me by reaching back to pat my leg. I wasn't sure how she managed it, because she was heavily pregnant herself and shifting around couldn't be that easy. "Women have been doing this for centuries. It's natural.

In the old days, women used to go out in the woods, squat down by the river, and just let it fly."

Dare met my gaze in his rearview mirror, and I wasn't sure which of us looked more wide-eyed. And he'd gone through childbirth before with his ex-wife.

"Shit, I'll have to be in the delivery room?"

"If I have to be in there, so do you." Rylee snatched the book back from me while I was lost in mental torment. "You play, you pay, pal. Just the circle of life. Also, my nipples aren't leaking."

"Mine do sometimes. But it's rare," Kelsey assured Dare as he cast her a sidelong look. "I still haven't figured out how I feel about breastfeeding. It's such a personal choice."

"You don't have to tell them about it," Dare informed her.

But Kelsey shrugged. "Eh, no shame in it. Why, at Baby Rama today, a woman just pulled out her breast in the stroller aisle and fed her kid. It's a beautiful, natural thing. Just requires that cow balm stuff because when they crack, sometimes there's bleeding and—"

I tuned her out for my own sanity. Also, she was my sister-in-law. I really did not need to think about the state of her nipples, whether or not she was speaking in hypotheticals.

By the time Dare dropped me and Rylee off at her apartment, he was obviously more than ready to drop Kelsey off at home and run back to the shop to hide in the comfort of broken carburetors and ailing transmissions. Anything was better than discussions of mucus and aching nipples and callused feet.

I still wasn't sure what the last one had to do with pregnancy, and I didn't want to know either.

Rylee went straight into the bathroom in her apartment and didn't come out for a while.

So, with more than a little trepidation, I picked up the book again. I would have to learn this stuff, right?

Besides, if Dare could deal with all of it, so could I.

Kelsey had said it was beautiful and natural.

Just like sex.

Right.

Within half a chapter, I tossed the book aside and went into the kitchen to search for a beer. Or any alcohol period. I knew Rylee couldn't drink right now, but she hadn't known that until a few days ago, and surely, she'd had some kind of liquor on hand for emergencies.

Yeah, that was a no.

Still, I looked through her fridge anyway just in case. Maybe a snack would help. Making a sandwich was methodical. And I might be panicked as fuck, but I could still eat.

Which was how I came upon the red Converse sneaker in the crisper. Next to a wilted head of lettuce.

Hmm.

I pulled it out and turned around just as Rylee stepped into the kitchen, rubbing her stomach.

"Well, guess it's time for the nausea part of our program—" She fell silent and frowned. "Why do you have my shoe?"

"The better question is why was it in your refrigerator?"

"It was not."

"Yes, it was."

"No, it wasn't."

"Ry, it was in there." I set the chilly footwear on the floor. "I've left my car keys in the freezer once or twice accidentally, but shoes are a new one, even for me."

"Wes must've did it," she said quickly.

Too quickly.

"My nephew puts shoes in refrigerators?"

Impatiently, she shook her head and picked up the shoe, transporting it across the apartment to the tidy mat by the front door where its mate waited innocuously. She set it down and dusted her hands. "You know kids. They mess around with stuff. He likes to... play pranks on me."

"Really? I didn't even realize you knew him that well."

She nodded and bit her lip, touching her stomach again. "I'm making an effort." Her voice sounded weak, and she'd gone even paler since she stepped out of the bathroom.

"Here, have a seat." I pulled her over to the couch and nudged her to sit down. "Do you want anything? I read that mint is good for settling the stomach."

"All I have is a mint air freshener."

"Hmm, probably not that." I thought back to the contents of her fridge. She didn't have much. "Want a water?"

"I can get it—"

"Sit."

I went to retrieve it and popped the cap before handing it over. She drank greedily, then wiped the back of her hand over her mouth. "That book should have a warning label or something. I'm half convinced that's what made me puke."

It shocked me how easy it was to laugh. Since, hey, I'd been traumatized too, but I wasn't the one who had a live action doll growing inside me. "It's a ton of information. A lot is going to happen to you." I blew out a breath. "To us."

"Yeah." She rubbed her fingers over the condensation on her bottle before setting it on the nearby table. "I'm sorry I've been...inconsistent."

I wasn't sure that would've been the word I would have chosen, but for right now, it was enough. "It's overwhelming. And you're right. We don't know each other that well. But we will."

"Yeah. You probably think I'm ungrateful, considering the whole money thing."

"You don't want me taking over your life. I get it."

"It's more like I hate feeling as if someone has to. Because I can't figure my shit out for myself, so what right do I have to bring a baby into it?"

"Rights or not, he or she is going to be here. And you might surprise yourself."

"Maybe. I hope so." She looked up at me under her lashes. "You're already surprising me. I guess I'm afraid I'm going to start depending on that—on you—and you're going to..."

"Take off?"

She nodded.

"Yeah, pretty sure my brother thinks the same. Your sister too." I scraped a hand over the back of my head. "Just means I'll have to work twice as hard to prove to everyone I can stick."

Even to myself.

"I get what it's like trying to convince people you can be different. And you never even did anything wrong. You got a lot right."

Her unexpected praise made me smile. "So did you."

She snorted. "Oh, yeah? Like what?"

"You rise to every challenge. Every time something knocks you down, huntress, you get back up."

"Yeah. I do." Lightly, she touched her belly. "Even bumpy areolas won't hold me down for long."

It felt good to laugh. "The book isn't all bad. There's a chart for how big the baby is at each stage."

Her throat moved. "Like weight and inches?"

"Yeah, in comparison to fruit." I sat down and reached out to touch her belly, then stopped with my hand halfway there. "May I?"

She nodded, her eyes huge.

I brushed my fingertips over her belly, and all at once, the scary shit invading my brain disappeared. There was just wonder and amazement and more than a little arousal at being this close to her again. "A plum," I said softly, swallowing hard. "Ours should be about the size of a plum right now."

"I like plums." She moved infinitesimally closer to me on the sofa.

I inched toward her as well, and we met in the middle. "Me too."

She tipped her head up to mine. "In case you're worried, my nipples really aren't leaking."

I had to grin. "Whew."

"And I brushed my teeth four times before I came out here. Did the mouthwash thing also."

"Good to know."

She glanced down at her chest, nicely outlined in her sweater. "As far as some of the other stuff I read, they seem the same color too."

"Did you check after you read that?"

"It would probably sound sexier to say yes, but I had to toss my cookies. Right afterward, I wasn't really focused on my nipples. But I checked myself out pretty thoroughly before I got dressed this morning, looking for any differences. My breasts weren't of note." She shifted toward me until her knees bumped mine.

"Speak for yourself."

Her lips twitched. "You appreciate them in a different way than I do."

"Damn straight." I sure as hell was appreciating them right now. Her nipples seemed to get harder the longer this conversation lasted.

"That whole sensitive thing—" She exhaled. "It's feeling like a factor right this second."

"Yeah?" I let my hand wander upward until I could cup the underside of her breast. They already felt fuller than they had in December, which had to be my imagination. Especially since I'd just been with her the other day and I hadn't noticed anything different.

Wishful thinking, maybe. Crazy, since she was already pretty damn perfect.

But I was already looking forward to seeing—and feeling—her body change. Even after flipping through that freaking book.

The human dick had amazing powers of restoration. Even near mental anguish wasn't enough to keep a good one down.

At least not when in the presence of Rylee Ford.

I rubbed my thumb over the stiff tip, and she shuddered. "Maybe I should check them out. See what's what. You know, for science."

Her lips curved as she sidled closer. "Maybe you should."

FIFTEEN

I WASN'T SURE THIS WAS A GOOD IDEA, BUT WHEN HE TOUCHED ME THE shouts of *omgamigoingtofuckthisup* went silent in my manic brain. And maybe even in my subconscious, because I'd slept relatively peacefully last night for the first time in a very long time.

It might have been the exhausted kind, but I officially had someone in my corner for the first time in what felt like forever.

I slid my fingers through his tightly shorn hair. Would our baby have curls? Is that why his was cut so ruthlessly short?

"Rylee."

"Hmm?"

"Where'd you go?"

I blinked up at him. "I'm right here."

"You were. And now not so much."

I smoothed my finger over the dense hair at his temple. "It wasn't bad. I was just wondering if you had curly hair when it's longer."

"Brillo pad status reporting for duty." He nibbled his way down my neck.

"I doubt it."

He pulled back and grinned at me. "There's a reason I learned how to use my own trimmer. Why?"

I shrugged. "Just wondering what kind of hair the baby will have."

"Oh." His eyes lost a little of the lust and went soft. "Kinda hope it's more like yours." He undid my braid and finger combed my hair. "Thick and soft. Somehow still shiny even though it's so dark."

"Like my dad's. My sister is the mailman's kid."

He gave me a half grin as he traced the backs of his fingers along my neck to the wide neck of my sweater. I shivered when he drifted over my breast again. "Just how sensitive are these?" He drew my sweater down to tongue my nipple through the flimsy material of my bra.

I tipped my head back and pushed them at him shamelessly. He moaned and the vibration kicked it up one more notch. The scruff of his rapidly growing beard made me hiss.

He grinned up at me. "Sensitive—check." He plucked at my nipple with his teeth until the snick of material releasing made me jolt.

I dragged his mouth up to mine and straddled his thighs. His hands immediately went to my ass and held me firm over his cock. There were far too many clothes between us, but right now, I needed to concentrate on his mouth before I did something crazy like dry hump him while he gave me an orgasm just by playing with my tits.

Was this a side-effect of pregnancy or just Gage?

Because while I enjoyed sex—a lot—it had never been like this before.

That first night had been intense and wild, but it could have just been the buzz of alcohol and loneliness.

Sure, Ry.

He ground me down on his cock and I sucked on his tongue like I would his cock later. Because there was no way I could wait to get him inside me. Maybe some of the overwhelming emotions careening through me would calm down with a little release.

I leaned back enough to flip my sweater off and he cupped my breasts while my hands were up over my head. I arched under the attention.

"So damn sensitive. Can I make you come just like this?"

I went for his belt. "Let's try with this."

He reached around for my clasp and tossed my bra away. "Let's slow down. Take our time."

"Why?"

He laughed. "Why not? Are you in a hurry?" He pushed my breasts together and went from one nipple to the other. Then he released them and pressed my hands to his chest. "Just enjoy."

I rolled my hips restlessly as he paid very close attention to...well, everything. His eyes watchful and patient as he found the combination of tugging, biting, and sucking that drove me insane. One hand slid up my neck, his thumb dipping into my mouth. My patience wore a little thin as I sucked him into my mouth, swirling my tongue around the pad of his finger.

Did he remember me doing that with the head of his cock?

That sensitive vein that ran under his shaft arrowing to the flared tip. So dark and tight. My mouth watered to get his taste on my tongue again.

He pinched a little harder than I was used to, but it knocked me over the edge. He latched his mouth to my breast, and I rode his bulge. I came with a surprised laugh and curled my arms around his neck. "God. You're terribly good at that."

"Terribly?" He groaned into my hair. "Gloriously is a better word."

"Well, you might have to bring your ego down a notch there, buddy."

"Is that right?" He twisted me back onto the couch and dragged off my leggings. "I'd say an over-the-clothes orgasm should get me a few compliments instead of insults."

I dragged him over me, wrapping my legs around his hips as I undid his belt. "Get that amazing cock out of your jeans. How's that?"

"Better." He groaned as I got a hold of his shaft. "Jesus, you make me as horny as a teenager."

"As long as you don't last like one."

"Hell, no." He growled my name as he thrust into my hand.

I dragged him down my swollen center and inside.

"Ry..." He groaned and stilled. "I'm not—"

"Think that's a bit of a non-issue. You know, already pregnant and all."

"Right." He pressed his forehead to mine and looked down at us. "But I've never… Sweet Jesus, you're so hot and perfect."

I smiled up at him and slowly took him into me. The way he stretched me dragged a low purr out of my throat. I rolled up to meet him and we learned how to…

God, was this what making love felt like?

I was used to the hot and wild. We'd had that from the start.

I reached up to cup his cheek, tipping his chin up to look at me, not our joined bodies. It would be easier to leave his attention there. I don't even know what possessed me to search for more.

Our eyes locked and sweat pooled between us as the sweet strokes became deeper and harder. He gripped the arm of the couch next to my head while he pushed my leg up to get a deeper angle.

"Gage."

He lowered his mouth to mine for a deep, hungry kiss before he curled his arm around me and swung me up to straddle him again. I braced myself on his shoulders and the angle was everything.

Intense. Infuriatingly intimate.

He reached up to grip my hair. "Rylee, I…"

I wrapped my arms around his neck and covered his mouth.

I didn't want to know if it was more. If the word that scared me most was on the tip of his tongue. It would be worse if it wasn't.

I sobbed into his mouth as his hands transferred to my hips. He pulled me down tight against him as he pulsed up inside me. The friction between us drove me over. I embraced the orgasm. I understood the chemistry between us. It was hormones, pheromones, and Gage was an insanely hot guy.

He held me tight as he came.

It was a new feeling. Safety was usually my number one concern. And yet this guy still had managed to get around a condom that first night we'd been together. Making the conscious effort to skip it was freeing and also made me realize it came with an extra drawback.

Cleanup.

I winced as he slid out of me, but instead of allowing it to get awkward, Gage stood up with me and stalked over to the bathroom. "I think a shower is in order."

I gripped his shoulders. "It's not a big shower."

"We'll make it work."

And we did. It included a lot of bumping and some cold spots while the two of us soaped up and tried to rinse off.

But I also got to get a look at him without the fogginess of lust. The strong shoulders and tapered waist. The number forty-four tattooed under his bicep, rather than on the outside of his arm like most guys did. It was prominent when he lifted his arm over his head to wash his hair.

I crowded into him, the stream of water sliding over his neck onto my chest. "Why did you leave racing?"

He kissed my nose. "It wasn't fun anymore."

"Pretty sure a job has times where it's not fun."

"I hit every goal I'd set out to do. I won races multiple times. Sponsors started jerking me around, wanting me to do crazy commercials and tell me what to wear." He ducked his head under the spray until the shampoo foamed around his shoulders and between us. He took my washing mitt and smoothed away the suds, adding my shower gel until there was nothing but the wildflower scent filling the steamy room.

"And that's it?"

"Pretty much. I drove across country because I'd said I always wanted to, but it was lonely. And seeing all the incredible places like the Grand Canyon and wineries in California didn't mean much when I was doing it by myself. Then my Camaro died."

"Really? Aren't you driving a Camaro now?"

"Bite your tongue. Stingrays are most certainly not the same. Especially to my baby who's now sitting in a storage unit."

"Terribly sorry. One penis car is the same is the next."

"You wound me, woman."

I slid my hand down to cup him. "Like I said before, you don't feel like you need to compensate for a little—"

His eyes flashed. "Watch it. Don't start that if you don't want me to finish it."

I grinned up at him. "Promises, promises."

"Oh, huntress. I'll turn you around and fuck you right into the tiled wall."

"Works for me." I gave him a firmer stroke. It was easier to do this than tell him I wouldn't mind being the passenger in his car. I'd never been farther than upstate New York and the occasional school trip when I was a kid.

He grinned. "I just bet."

"So, rather than race cars, now you're just going to play dad with me?" I smoothed away the fuzz of soap on his pecs, my pinkie scoring his nipple lightly.

He caught my hand, holding it over his heart. "I'm not going to play at it. I want to be a good father. I want our kid to know I'm here for her or him." He tipped my chin up with his other hand and our gazes met. "That I'm here for his mom."

I blinked away the rush of tears. Was I just a mom?

Even if that was all that was truly between us, it was more than I'd ever had.

I smiled because he needed me to. And I had to, or I'd ask questions I shouldn't. It was bad enough they were already pushing at me this soon. What was it about him? Was it just the pregnancy hormones flexing inside of me? Searching out for the family and the whole nesting thing Kelsey spoke about?

"Well, if you're serious."

"I am."

I released him and caught my mitt between us. "I talked to my sister about doctors."

"Oh, good. That's smart."

"I have my moments."

He twisted our fingers together. "More than a few."

"If I called to make an appointment, maybe you could go with me?"

"Yes. Definitely. Just tell me when and where."

The lust had faded, and only the sweet guy I was getting to know remained. "Thanks."

He cupped my face. "No need to thank me. I want to be there for you and the baby. Even if it means going to scary doctor's offices."

I wrapped my fingers around his arms. "I'll take you up on it, because I'm scared shitless."

He kissed me firmly. Not in the way that meant we were going to stay naked, which I would have been cool with, to tell the truth. Sex was easy to understand. Even if he kept turning the tables on me.

This was different. Now he was speaking in a more resolute tone that actually reminded me of Dare.

"Let's get you fed, and we'll have a relaxed night in. How's that sound?"

"Does that mean Netflix and chill?"

He smirked down at me. "It could."

"I'm down for that."

"Yeah?" Tenderly, he brushed my wet hair away from my cheek. "Me too."

SIXTEEN

"When I said feed you, this isn't what I had in mind."

She looked up from her loaded bagel. We were sitting in Brewed Awakening as Macy and her crew were cleaning up. "I don't even have to wear a bra down here. No one is here but us girls."

"First of all, hello—not a girl."

She grinned around a crunchy bite.

"And I'm well aware you're not wearing a bra. You're trying to kill me."

Her eyes twinkled as she licked cream cheese and jam from the side of her hand.

"That's gross."

"Don't knock it till you try it." She ripped off a piece and held it out to me.

I took her wrist and licked the blackberry jam from her thumb. Her chewing slowed and her dark eyes got that look. The one that made me want to toss her over my shoulder and drag her back upstairs.

But that wouldn't help us get to know one another.

I knew she kept slotting me in the sperm donor role. I wanted her to see I was more than that. I needed more than that. And that meant I needed to keep my dick in my pants for at least most of the night.

God save me.

I took the piece of bagel and huffed out a surprised moan.

"Good, right?"

"That sweet and savory thing. I'm a fan."

She smiled as she took another bite. "I know, right?"

"Is that a craving thing? Or you just like it?"

"No. One of my roommates was from England. Seems they do this on English muffins. Also delicious. Of course I don't think they call them the same thing."

"Just a muffin?"

She wrinkled her nose. "Smart ass."

"Anyway, she got me to try it. It took me longer to say yes, by the way."

"I pretty much like most food, unlike my brother. And traveling all over, I learned that weird food didn't always mean bad. Though some of it really does. Grits? Yeah, still a hard pass no matter how my buddies dress them up down south."

"Texture," we both said in unison.

"Exactly." I picked up my toasted cheese sandwich. I was going to look like one. I pretty much ate it every other day since I'd had lunch with Rylee that first day I was in town. Hard to believe so much had changed so fast.

I swallowed hard as Ry licked her thumb again. "Sure that bagel is enough?"

"I'm going to bribe Macy for some of her sweet and savory popcorn mix."

"So that's a thing then?"

She shrugged. "I guess. I never really thought about it, but I have been eating a lot of sweet and salty things lately."

"Speaking of."

"All baby, all the time, Kramer."

"I was just thinking about the parents' thing. We should tell them. Maybe together?"

Her brows lifted. "Hey, mom. Meet my baby mama Rylee."

I reached across the table and covered her hand. "Would you stop with that? You're more than that to me. I don't think you get that."

She started to pull her hand away, but I held it tight. "Why?"

"Why not? You're bright, funny, stupidly beautiful, and we clicked since that very first night."

"We clicked at the hips, Gage."

"It was before that and you know it. I saw you across that bar and went right to you."

She swallowed. "Because of my short skirt."

Dammit, she was a stubborn woman. What the hell did I have to do to get her to see I wasn't just about the sex? "You weren't wearing a skirt. It was jeans. Perfect, snug jeans and a sparkly T-shirt thing that showed just a little slice of your tanned stomach."

Her eyes widened. "That was three months ago."

"It was worth remembering."

"You guys okay?" Macy hollered from the counter of the café.

I huffed out a breath. "Yeah, we're just finishing up."

Macy came around the half wall that sectioned off the reading nook. Pink and yellow pumpkins were stashed everywhere in the little section. She had a spray bottle and rag in her hands.

Rylee popped the last of her bagel in her mouth. "Thanks for letting us come in so late."

"Sure. I can clean around you."

"Do you think we could stay down here and watch a movie?"

Macy's eyebrow arched. She glanced from me back to Rylee.

"I mean, we don't have to. It was just an idea." Rylee rushed on at Macy's look.

"No, that's cool. Just text me when you're done, and I'll put the security on."

"We don't want to keep you up late." I played with Rylee's suddenly stiff fingers.

"I don't sleep." Macy swiped Rylee's plate and gave me a look, and when I held up my hands, she took mine too. "Have fun. You know where the remotes are."

"I do. Thanks, Mace."

"You got it."

"Oh, one more thing?"

"Popcorn too, you heathen?"

"Yes, please."

Macy sighed. "All right. But only because I like you," she said over her shoulder. "And my popcorn is legendary enough to show it off."

Rylee stood up. "Wait until you see this setup." Instead of detangling our fingers, she pulled me over toward the L-shaped couch in the corner of the reading section. She tapped the side of the end table and a secret compartment opened. She hit a button on the remote and a huge screen lowered from the ceiling.

"Whoa."

"Yeah. Awesome, right?"

I settled next to her and had to smile when she burrowed right into me without getting riled up about me being in her space. And the fact that she fit me so well made something deep inside my chest expand. Even if I had to watch a romantic comedy, I wouldn't trade this for anything.

When the projector came up and the movie selection included every horror movie I'd ever seen or heard of in my life, I laughed.

"What? You a pussy, Gage?"

"Hell, huntress." I grinned down at her. "The scarier the better."

She settled in and rested her hand on my belly. "Damn right."

Macy came back with a huge bowl of popcorn and two orange sodas.

Rylee sat up a little. "Thanks, Mom."

"Fuck off."

"Love you too," she called after Macy, who flipped her the bird as she stalked toward the back of the café. "She's such a softie."

"Yeah, if you mean tiger claws with a left hook."

She picked at the sinful popcorn. "More like a baseball bat."

"And you know this how?" I stole the piece she was aiming for and she narrowed her eyes at me.

"Hey."

I held it in front of her mouth.

She opened her lips and nipped my fingers as she took it. Before she was done chewing, I lowered my mouth to take a taste. Caramel and cheddar cheese never tasted so good. She pushed me back against the couch. "I'm watching a movie, sir."

I looked around. "It's a pretty cool setup."

"Yeah." She fiddled with the bowl.

"What?"

She shrugged and blew out a sigh.

I told my cock to take a chill pill, but the *sir* thing had stirred things it should not have. She obviously had something on her mind. "What're you thinking about?"

"It's nothing."

I twisted to her and set the bowl behind me. "Obviously not when I can hear your brain whirling from here."

"Ever since I sat down here with Macy to watch a movie I wondered if other people would enjoy the same thing. There's not much to do in Crescent Cove after oh, seven o'clock."

I laughed. "Things do seem to close up early."

"Even the pizza place is closed before nine."

I grinned. "Yeah, my pops isn't exactly a late-night guy."

"Oh." She blinked. "Right. I sort of forgot about that part."

"That my dad owns the pizza joint?"

"Yeah. Sorry. I didn't mean anything by it."

I toyed with her fingers. "Our families have kind of crashed together without a lot of time for Christmas dinners."

"Yeah, ain't that the truth. Both of Kelsey's weddings were thrown together last minute." She laced her fingers with mine. "I made an awesome impression too."

I turned her hand so I could nip at her wrist. "Helluva story for our grandkids."

Her eyebrows shot up. "Kids?"

"Who knows? And no, beyond my pops's store, there isn't much of a night life here."

She blew out a breath. "No. And once the initial rush is over, people sort of just hang out in the café."

"As one does."

"I know but look at all the space in here. What if we had a few projection screens? The one over here, and maybe next door. There's a bunch of space to expand." Her eyes brightened and she started to rev up with excitement. "Maybe a patio out back. I mean, it might not be feasible with second-run movies since they're still pretty expensive. At least when I looked it up online."

"So, you've looked into it?"

She looked down at our hands. "Unemployed and insomniac means lots of web browsing. But like in the summer, on a patio watching some old movies. Doesn't have to be horror, though I bet there's a case for them with the two schools we have on the outer edges of the lake."

"And *Halloween* is making a comeback. Maybe old slasher movie nights. Do a theme?"

She leaned into me. "Yeah. And you tasted that popcorn. What if I could get Macy to whip up a recipe and we could make them in mass quantities. And Vee is a baker by trade. She makes most of the stuff in the little bakery section they have. But we also have Sugar Rush down the street. Maybe work with them and a few other places in town to use it like a sales area too."

"You've really been thinking about this." It wasn't a question. I knew she was too smart to be working for someone. I dug my phone out of my pocket. "I saw this really cool couch on my buddy's Facebook page." I flicked through my feed and found his profile, then went through the pictures posted. "There it is." I handed her the phone.

She enlarged the picture and chewed on her bottom lip. "That looks really expensive."

"Well, Brian has a lot of money to burn. But you just so happen to know a guy who's good with cars. Hell, there's a half car in the junkyard at JT's. A little buff and shine and a redo of the cushions..." I felt the twinge again.

The same one I'd felt looking at the old Ford in the junkyard.

She peered up at me. "You could build that?"

I nodded. I could see the wheels spinning in her head. "You should talk to Macy about it. See how she feels." I nodded to the menu screen full of movies. "Obviously, you have similar interests."

"You should see the collection of horror and *Grindhouse* memorabilia she has hidden in with the mugs over in those cubbies."

"I know." I laughed. "I bought a travel mug with Michael Myers on it."

"Good taste." Her eyes sparkled, then dimmed almost immediately. "I probably shouldn't. I don't know anything about running a business."

"How many different kinds of jobs have you had?"

She blew out a laugh. "Ran out of fingers and toes. See? That's not a woman who should run a business."

"Or it's the perfect one who should. You know how to deal with people."

"I also have a temper."

"I know you do. Freaking hot."

She punched my arm. "Shut up."

"No, really, Ry. You should talk to Macy."

"I—"

"Do your research. Make up a business plan." I laughed at her face. "If it isn't still interesting even after you look at it for real, then you'll find something else to do." I brushed my thumb over the wrinkle between her brows. "I know you will."

"Oh, yeah with a baby on the way."

"Some people need a time limit. You know you have a few months to figure stuff out."

"I still need a job, Gage."

"You want to work at another flower shop? Or at the school?"

"No."

I laughed at the way she pouted. "Is it an imperative?"

"No. I have quite a bit of savings to be honest."

"Enough to build a business?"

She settled back into the couch. "If I was careful."

"Think about it."

"Maybe."

And that had to be good enough, but the seeds were planted. I didn't know what the hell I was doing, but it was easier to see it as an outsider to Rylee's ideas. For someone with such a forceful personality, she played it very carefully in some ways. Maybe not so unlike her sister in that regard.

I reached for the huge popcorn bowl and put it back on our laps. "Ready for that movie?"

She fit herself back against my side, her eyes gleeful as she lifted the remote.

Twenty minutes later, we were both engrossed in the classic slasher movie. We started with *Friday the 13th,* but quickly discovered a mutual love for the *Halloween* movies.

By the time we moved on into the lesser sequel, Rylee started nodding off. I couldn't blame her. It had been a damn long day. She murmured lightly against my chest. I settled her more comfortably against me. Would be just my luck she'd have a nightmare.

Though it didn't seem her style. Especially not with that list of horror movies she'd watched.

She settled down when I rubbed light circles along the base of her neck. Her warmth and the very long day had me dozing off as well. The lights were low in the café and the couch was comfortable as fuck. I'd never been averse to cuddling. Being alone in a car for most of my day, or around a bunch of hardcore racing guys, made a guy crave a softer touch.

And I'd been craving it for a long damn time.

My lifestyle didn't allow for it. Always traveling, always stressing over the next big race. Endless parties and sponsor driven glad-handing. I was so done with it all. The quiet of Crescent Cove was exactly what I'd run from. Now I craved it.

And this woman next to me.

Suddenly, Rylee sat up and took the bowl off the table.

"Ry?"

She didn't answer me. She just seemed to shuffle off, bumping into chairs and tables like a pinball. Left, right, straight—then she went right into the café and behind the counter.

I popped up off the couch. "Rylee?"

"Just have to make the coffee. It's okay."

"Coffee? Now? Are you supposed to have that anyway?" I wound around the chairs she'd bumped in the process.

"Of course I am. I have to get ready for work."

Work? She didn't have a job right now.

She set the large bowl in the bakery case on top of the wrapped brownies. I frowned. What the hell?

I moved around her, but her eyes were glassy. I stepped back as she went to the drawer at the center of the counter and pulled out a knife.

Yeah, we were not going for a knife after watching Michael Myers.

I glanced at the bakery case and suddenly, the red sneaker in her crisper made so much sense. I raked my fingers through my hair.

My girl was a sleepwalker.

Well, shit.

"Uh-oh."

I spun around to the voice. "Oh, shit. I…um. Just give me a second—"

Macy held up her hand. She was dressed in black pants and a huge football jersey with Garfield stepping on Odie's neck on the front. I was pretty sure the original cartoonist hadn't sanctioned the shirt. Especially since the iconic dog's eyes were zombified and Garfield was carrying a bat that looked eerily like the one Negan carried from *The Walking Dead*. "No need. It's how we became friends."

I frowned. "What?"

Macy shook her head and did a light step around Rylee, taking the knife and jar of peanut butter jar out of reach. When my girl went for a canister of sugar, Macy cursed. "I swear she's getting better at this."

"You know about this?"

Macy shifted her armful of kitchen accessories to a shelf behind her. "Yep."

I looked around. "How did you know she was..." I was completely at a loss.

"Cameras. I have them on a sensor trigger for my little felon."

"And you're not freaked?"

She laughed. "Nope. I did some reading up on it. Evidently, you're not really supposed to wake them up if you can avoid it. Just kind of steer them back to bed. Since we're not exactly close to her bedroom, I'm gonna have to wake her up."

"Should I do it?"

Macy looked up at me, then tilted her head. "Hmm."

I wasn't sure what that meant, but Rylee was starting to make a little keening sound that snapped my attention back to her. I crossed to her. Just as I was about to touch her arm, Macy cleared her throat. I looked back at her.

"I wouldn't." She waved me over to her. "Supposedly, a loud noise from a distance is the best way to wake them. Gives them time to get orientated."

It went against every instinct inside me, but I backed up to stand beside Macy. "You know a lot about this."

She shrugged.

"No other details?"

"Not my story to share."

I huffed out a breath. "How many times—"

"Ask Rylee, not me."

I locked my hands behind my neck. I didn't like feeling helpless. The longer Rylee bounced from counter to counter in confusion, the more upset she got.

I slapped my hand down on the counter beside me.

She stopped moving.

I did it again, and she swayed.

"Fuck this." I crossed the space in two strides and caught her against me. "Hey, you." I kept my voice soft.

She looked up at me, her eyes soft and sleepy. "Gage?"

"Yeah, baby. It's me."

Her eyebrows lowered and then her eyes widened. "No." Her eyes filled, and she pushed out of my arms. "God, no."

"Ry, wait."

She glanced at Macy then back at me and her face crumpled. She raced around the counters and bakery case to the main part of the café and out the side door that led to the apartments.

"Dammit."

"Let her go."

"No, I can't let her go. She's upset."

"She's embarrassed. Same as she was the first time I caught her doing it."

"I thought you weren't going to say how it happened," I growled.

"Don't get shitty with me because you're angry. Give her a bit to calm down."

I let out a breath. "No, she's been running away from me for long enough."

SEVENTEEN

I RACED UP THE STAIRS TO MY APARTMENT.

I hadn't done that the night before. I'd been so stupid to think maybe I was settling down again. Why did it have to be in front of Gage? That careful tone of his voice. The confusion in his eyes.

I knew what was coming next. The stammering, the race for the door. Or even worse, kind words followed directly by pity.

The worst was when they tossed the nice card around. As if Hallmark could make a slogan for this.

Hey, sorry you don't know how to sleep like a normal person. Good luck with that and see ya around.

God, I couldn't even write a good card description in my head.

I went for the cupboard above the fridge for my hidden bottle of whiskey then shoved it in the sink when I remembered that couldn't happen. The glass shattered in the sink because of course it wasn't the cheap shit.

If I was going to drink, it was worth the time and effort.

I stalked around my tiny kitchen as embarrassment flowed into anger. Why now? We were just starting to...

What?

Sort of click? Not just at the waist. We'd laughed over the movies and I'd even told him about my ideas for the movie screening nights I wanted to talk to Macy about. Especially when she brought out the popcorn and Gage got a firsthand look at how fun it could be.

He'd seemed excited for me.

Not writing me off.

And now this?

I didn't have time to ease him into my dirty little secret.

"Ry?"

My eyes burned at the sound of his voice. Maybe if I stayed quiet, he'd think I went to bed. Though he knew firsthand that I didn't fucking stay there.

He knocked. "Come on, Rylee. I know you're in there."

I went over to the door, but I couldn't bring myself to turn the doorknob. I didn't want to see the pity on his face. The *poor Rylee* expression in his eyes right before he walked.

Just like Shane.

At least this time I didn't do it in the middle of the quad. Heck, I could go and do it in the gazebo to show the whole damn town. Did they make industrial locks to protect a person from themselves?

He slapped his hand against the door. "You're going to make me do this through the door?"

I pressed my forehead to the smooth wood, aching to undo the locks keeping him out.

"Okay, if that's the way you want it."

I braced myself, the tears dripping down my stupid face. He'd go back down the stairs and head out. Back to his folks' house?

I didn't even know where he was staying. I just didn't ask. Not wanting to see him in any kind of permanent status with this town—or with me.

"You surprised me, huntress. Being all kinds of a coward over something so stupid."

I straightened and swiped away tears. What the hell did he mean that I was a coward?

"This just makes you even more interesting."

I unlocked the door and swung it open. "What?"

He gripped the top of the doorjamb, his posture lazy and sexy. Just like the first time I saw him. "Yes. Do you know how much I can fuck with you? I can whisper shit in the dark—maybe I can get you to even —*ooof*."

I jammed my fist into his belly. "You asshole."

He reached inside and hauled me up against him. "You don't want to hear what I want you to do?"

"No, you pervert." I didn't laugh. I didn't want to be charmed.

"How could you think so little of me?"

"Because you're male." I tried to push out of his arms, but he held me tight.

"Really, Ry." He touched his forehead to mine. "You think this matters?"

I tried to twist away, and he tucked his hands into the back pockets of my ancient jeans. "Gage..."

"No. This is not our deal breaker."

"I'm a freak." I stared at his neck because I couldn't look at his face.

"No, you're not." He shook me. "Look at me. Dammit, Ry."

I snapped my gaze to his.

"You have a hugely active mind that doesn't know how to sleep laying down in a damn bed. Why does that make you a freak?"

"Hello? You saw me."

"Do you know what you did?"

My face heated. No. I never remembered what I was doing. Whatever I was dreaming about didn't stay with me when I woke up. It was like two different planes almost.

"You walked across the room. Put a bowl of popcorn in a bakery case. That's about it."

I frowned. "I felt like I was doing more."

"Well, you kind of did go for a knife."

"Oh, God."

"Not sure what else you were looking for. Hopefully, not my head."

"Peanut butter."

"Come again?"

I sighed. "Peanut butter. I'm going to be three-hundred pounds by the end of this pregnancy. It's all I keep finding—peanut butter knives in the drawer and sink. I've gone through multiple jars of the stuff since I moved in."

"Could it be part of the pregnancy thing? You know, how you were wanting sweet and salty flavors. Peanut butter certainly fits the definition."

I relaxed in his hold. "Maybe."

He eased me farther inside and closed the door, then he took my hand and led me to the couch. "Okay. Let's talk about this."

I perched at the edge of the couch. "Talk about what? I sleepwalk, end of story."

"Somehow I doubt it."

I twisted my hand free and clutched them together between my knees. "I used to do it as a kid. My doctor said I'd grow out of it. Just gave my parents some tips on how to deal with it. And I did grow out of it." For a while. Unless I was crazy stressed.

"And…"

I flopped back on the couch. "And then it came back when I was in college."

He winced.

"Yeah, as bad as you're thinking, times it by one hundred."

"Ah, babe." He shifted closer to me until our knees bumped.

"Yeah, I wanted to finish college. I was a freshman and stressed out. I was dating a nice guy. He thought the sleepwalking thing was cute. I didn't do anything other than talk in my sleep a little. Sometimes tried to get ready for class in the middle of the night. He'd just put me back in bed and I'd go back to sleep."

"Until you didn't, I'm guessing?"

That night was still burned in my memory. Not the dream—no, that was still stubbornly gone. But the embarrassment of the moment? Yeah, that was etched in my brain forever.

"Try middle of the quad at two in the morning while a party was going on."

"Shit."

"Oh, yeah." I gave a surprised grunt when he hauled me over his lap and hugged me to him. I rested my hands on his chest. "Gage."

"I'm sorry, huntress. That had to be the worst. Not just doing it, but at a party. I can't even imagine."

I relaxed against him. I'd never really told anyone what happened. There were witnesses of course, but the particulars had always been mine. I'd told my parents I was sleepwalking, and it was enough for me to beg to come home.

"And the worst part? Shane was at the party. It was a big Greek night, but I had my mid-term the next morning, so I'd skipped the party."

He hooked his thumbs in my back pockets in the lazy, possessive way I was growing used to. "Probably not really psyched about that either."

I hadn't really thought of that before. I'd been too focused on the embarrassment. "Actually, you're probably right. Maybe even why I ended up at the party. Too bad I didn't put pants on."

"Fuck."

"Oh, yeah."

"Hey, eighteen-year-old Rylee probably had amazing legs. They're damn fine now."

I laughed. "Ass."

He leaned forward and kissed me around the laugh I couldn't stop.

"So, I lived with my parents for years after that."

"Did you go see someone? A specialist? Like those sleep studies they do for people. I think my friend's dad had to do an overnight stay for something."

"Apnea?"

He shrugged. "Maybe."

"I did one when I was younger. It was awful." Being hooked up to machines and trying to sleep. It had been a nightmare. "I just dealt with it."

He frowned. "Just like that?"

"It took a few years. My dad jerry-rigged a sensor on the door. But I usually got around it. I'm some sort of Houdini when I'm asleep."

"Ah. That makes sense. Macy wouldn't say anything about why she knew."

My eyes stung again. "She's a really good friend." I cleared my throat and dabbed at my eyes. Crying wasn't going to help. "I hadn't been sleepwalking for a long time. I never could find a job I loved, but I saved because my mom and dad wouldn't let me pay rent. And I got the job here. I thought it was time to grow up, you know? Go out on my own."

"And your doctor never told you why you did it?"

I dashed away the last of my stupid tears. "They never had a definitive answer. Hormones, just luck of the draw."

He lifted a hand to cup my face. "Well, pregnancy might cover it."

I laughed. "Ya think?"

"Maybe we can ask the baby doctor? You can't be the only one this has ever happened to." He dropped his hand to my middle. "And we have a little more to worry about now than just embarrassing you with some peanut butter. What if you fell down the stairs? Or worse, went out the front door?"

I dipped my head. "I know. I have my cup trick."

"Cup trick?"

"Yeah. I try to set little booby traps for myself. That's the Houdini thing I was talking about. Somehow since I'm the one who did the trap..."

"Your subconscious knows how to get around it."

It sounded insane to say it out loud. "Still don't think I'm a freak?"

"I think you're a fucking genius, even in your sleep."

"Genius felon, if you ask Macy."

"Tell you what. I'll set the trap tonight, huh?"

I sat back and slid off his lap. "Really?"

"Yeah. I used to be really good at doing some stealthy shit against Dare. Did you know Legos hurt like a bitch if you step on them?"

I laughed. "Um, no. Me and Kelsey were more into Barbies and drawing paper."

"Well, if you step on those suckers in your sleep, you're definitely waking up."

"Gage?"

"Hmm?"

"Where are we going to find Legos?"

"Guess we're going shopping tomorrow." He stood up and dragged me to my feet. "Tonight will be a kamikaze maze of cups."

"Why are you being so...I don't know...cool about this?"

"It's a problem we'll figure out together, that's all. It's not about being cool about it." He slid his arms around me. "I don't want anything to happen to you. I just found you, dammit."

I curled my arms around his neck and held on tight. I'd never had anyone just hold me. Worried glances between my parents were a staple for sure, but just holding me and telling me it was all right?

Yeah, not so much.

Every damn thing was new territory with this man. And I was growing to care more about him by the minute.

EIGHTEEN

I WAS ABOUT TO SWITCH ALLEGIANCES WITH REALTORS. IF OLIVER showed me one more new build, I was going to toss him into Crescent Lake. With a small prayer, I tapped in the address into my GPS and headed out.

A ten-minute drive from town should make Rylee happy at least.

When I finally told her I was house hunting.

Sweet Jesus, I hope she didn't try to de-ball me. Ever since I'd gotten her fired, she'd been stressing about her job situation. I wanted to take care of her, but she was hellbent on the independent woman action.

Which I appreciated…in theory. Until she thwarted me at every turn.

However, I had won the Legos argument that first night and the ones since. I was pretty in tune with her now that I stayed at her place most nights, but one night she did get up without me noticing. Probably because I'd been up late the night before and sleeping a little more soundly than I usually did.

She'd stepped through my Legos landmine and swore a blue streak. It sure as shit woke her up. Point one for the Kramer camp.

I was still in the losing column. Considering I'd started off that way with our first meeting, it wasn't all that surprising.

From the first bet, she'd been one-upping me. And had been ever since.

Rylee hadn't been kidding about her peanut butter obsession. I was ready to get a Costco membership just to keep up with her.

Christ, me and a wholesale membership. Wasn't that a fucking kick? But I was ready for it. My mom kept tearing up every time she saw me thanks to our family dinner the other night.

Breaking the news to them felt much like I was a teenager telling my mom and dad a rubber broke, but I was pretty sure Dare had already broken them in on the shock factor. He'd done it twice.

But in my mom's mind, it meant I was sticking around. Hence the tears every five minutes. Oh, and the random onesies she kept showing me whenever I came home to do laundry. She was firmly in the "it's a girl" camp. I was pretty sure Rylee was too.

During our doctor's appointment, she'd just wanted to make sure the baby was healthy. I wanted to know the actual sex of the baby. I figured I should know if I needed to buy a shotgun or an extra racing helmet.

Though knowing my luck with the fairer sex, if I did have a girl, she'd probably be the next Danica Patrick just to make me insane.

Then I'd need shotguns and valium.

Telling Rylee's mom and dad had been a little more of an ulcer-inducing affair. Especially for me because Ry didn't want to tell them her sleepwalking was a problem again. There'd been some disappointment and worry between them. Add in the grilling I had endured from her father, and I felt like I'd been on the last lap of a very shitty race by the end of the dinner.

Not to mention the "What are your intentions toward my daughter" daggers I got through the meal from Mr. Ford. I had not been invited to call him Doug. I wanted to reassure them that my sole goal was to get Rylee to see me as the forever guy she needed. Unfortunately, she'd been quick to throw me under the bus.

Independent woman.

I'd said curse words with less vehemence lately.

She was so worried about telling everyone she could handle everything, I was left on the sidelines looking like a chump half the time.

So, here I was doing a secret house hunting spree to make sure she knew I was serious. I wasn't fucking going anywhere. What said that more than buying a damn house?

I pulled up behind the SUV at the bottom of the drive. It was a long driveway which I liked. Less chance of Rylee making it down to the road. I hated to think that way—in fact, I'd even looked into a special security system used by Alzheimer's patients to prevent them from wandering.

Only I was trying to keep a woman subconsciously running from me.

Helluva thing.

I climbed out of my car and tilted my head at the pretty swanky SUV. It still made my palms sweat a little at the thought of driving a family car versus a sports car, but not as much as it would have a few months ago. My, how things had changed in my life.

Oliver Hamilton climbed out of his SUV with a shark smile. I liked him. He wasn't quite as affable as his brother, but he was no nonsense about house hunting, and I appreciated that. I hated the sales schtick that most realtors laid on thick.

I'd almost bought a house twice in my life. Once for an investment. Tax brackets and some other BS from my accountant had dented my party brain for a half a second. Being on the road all the time got tiresome and my trailer felt more like a home than even my old hometown. But then my sponsorship had changed, and I'd been distracted with even more time on the road.

It seemed stupid to put down roots when I'd never actually be in the house.

And the other had been when I'd made my first million. Buying a house seemed the thing to do. Instead, I'd bought a ridiculous apartment in Manhattan, selling it for a loss within a year.

Gun-shy? Who, me?

Now there was a new life change sitting on my shoulders. I had more boxes to check this time around. Just not ones I had planned on.

Oliver came at me with an outstretched hand. "You didn't want a new build. I'd say this definitely applies."

I shook his hand and took off my sunglasses. "No, definitely not new." The stone house was close to the lake, but not right on top of it. All I needed to do was stress myself into a straitjacket about Rylee sleepwalking into the water. Followed directly by a drowning child.

But the land went on forever.

"Six acres."

I whistled.

"Yes, it's a miracle this hasn't been bought up by one of the developers who have been picking at the coastline for the last year. As soon as it went on the market, I called you."

"It's gorgeous."

"The house is a ranch style. It was renovated five years ago by the previous owners. I think you'll like it. It's move-in ready."

"I like the sound of that." I followed him up the gravel drive that turned into cement.

Oliver gave me the breakdown on the county roads and snow removal. It had been a damn long time since I'd had to worry about such things, but I was back in the snow belt.

The yard went on for...well, acres. There was plenty of flat ground for a kid, maybe even kids, to run around. The little buzz I'd been waiting for started humming at the back of my neck.

It was the same buzz that hadn't steered me wrong since I started my career.

There was a sturdy fence keeping the house separated from the lake. "Is the dock mine—part of the land?"

Way to be cool, Gage.

"Yes, the dock is included in the sale."

At least Oliver had the good graces not to smirk at me.

The front door was huge. Obviously upgraded for that whole curb appeal all the *House Hunter*-type shows and magazines harped on. The porch and front yard were manicured way past what I was capable of, but the idea of a riding mower all tricked out with some extra chrome increased the buzz factor once again.

Oliver rattled off more stats about the size of the house, the five bedrooms, and the bonus rooms. All I saw was a huge kitchen with lots of interesting surfaces and wide-open spaces. And windows letting in crazy light.

I saw kids running around.

I saw Rylee laughing as she convinced me to get the largest television possible for her horror movies.

Space to grow and a blank canvas for her to make it hers as much as mine.

I saw a life I'd never dared to dream about.

"I want it."

Oliver stopped talking. "You made it about three minutes longer than I thought you would."

I shook my head. "You're an asshole."

Oliver lifted a careless shoulder. "The house on Robinson was perfect for you—" He held up his hand at me. "But since you seem to have this one-story requirement, I found you this one."

"And I appreciate it. I'll take it."

"I haven't even shown you the bedrooms."

"I don't really care. There's windows and light, right? Lots of space."

"The master suite is quite stupendous. Come on, it'll just take a minute."

My phone buzzed in my pocket. And since I had a pregnant girlfriend…ish person in my life, I didn't leave messages unchecked like I used to.

I'm here. Where are you?

I grinned at the text and replied.

I texted you weeks ago.

I had a thing.

I shook my head. Tish always had a thing. She was one of the most in-demand fabricators I'd ever known. Probably because she could literally create anything given enough time and a damn pencil.

And in those few weeks, I'd found out I was going to be a father and I'd fallen hard for a stubborn woman with so much light in her eyes it made me wonder how I'd walked away from her in the first place.

Mostly because she'd kicked me in the teeth with her one and done nonsense. Nothing on this fucking planet needed to happen once when it came to us. It needed to be repeated thousands of times. Well, maybe with the kid thing we could slow it down to two, maybe three.

But with Tish in town, perhaps I'd take the second opinion on the house.

"Yeah, show me the bedrooms." I quickly texted Tish the address and asked her to come by.

I got a middle finger reply, followed by a thumbs up.

"Mind if I have a friend come and take a look?"

"I've got you slated for an hour. Plenty of time."

"Lead the way then."

I followed him through the long hallways to the bathrooms. One was something called a Jack and Jill since it connected two of the bedrooms. Then at the back of the house was the master suite.

Whistling would cover it.

"Holy Jesus."

"I know."

I gave Oliver a side-eyed glance and ignored the smugness coming off him. There was a huge window showcasing the lake and a view that made my chest ache and maybe added a slightly shaky stutter to my heart. "That's a million-dollar view."

"Not quite."

Well, if it was under a million, at least I could feed my kid for a few years without worrying about what kind of job I was going to create for myself.

And if I had to buy JT's Auto Body without my brother.

I didn't want to, but I would.

I just had to do a little bit of fancy footwork to get some things to fall into line. And anything had to be easier than getting Rylee to agree with me on what color the sky was and if we were having a boy or a girl.

We were looking at the third bedroom when the rumble of a motorcycle progressively got closer.

Oliver gave me a raised brow. "Your friend."

"Indeed."

"Do we need to go down—"

"Holy fuck, Gage. This is a goddamn palace!"

"Guess we don't need to go down and let her in."

I laughed. "No. Not sure there's a lock that can keep Tish out if you even engaged one."

"I did not."

"Well, that's good."

Her booted heels clomped down the hardwood floors as she stalked through the space. "Buy it. If you don't, I need to find me a sugar daddy to buy it for me. Well, hello there. Possible sugar daddy?"

Oliver blinked and quickly waved his wedding ring finger. "Taken."

"Damn. Looking for a side piece?"

"What my friend means is hello and nice to meet you." I gave her a hard stare.

Tish flipped a flame-red lock of hair over her shoulder. She was wearing a heavy, armored motorcycle jacket over leather pants and five-inch heels. Not that she needed them. She was just a few inches shorter than me, but she liked to lord herself over men in general.

She held out her hand to Oliver. He hesitated but shook her hand. "Tish Burns."

"Nice to meet you, Ms. Burns."

She gave a great booming laugh. "Is this guy for real?" She hooked her thumb at Oliver. "You sure you don't want to go for a ride, handsome? I bet I can get you call me Tish without all that formality crap."

"I'm quite sure."

"His wife would kill you, Tish."

"Oh, yeah? Think I might need to meet a girl like that."

Oliver cleared his throat. "I bet you'd like to see the master suite."

She hooked her arm through his. "I sure would."

Oliver shot a slightly panicked look over his shoulder at me. Man, I'd missed Tish. She would like Rylee, I was almost sure. Who wouldn't like her?

Yeah, I was biased. And happy.

Everything was falling into place. Now all I had to do was get my brother on board with the three of us starting a business.

NINETEEN

I PICKED UP THE STACK OF DISHES ON THE SIDE TABLE IN THE READING nook. It was becoming my permanent residence lately. I had the want ads open in the local paper, as well as a number of online applications half-filled, but Gage's words kept encroaching on my poor brain.

I wanted to talk to Macy about maybe expanding. Maybe just helping out to start. She was so busy all the time and she and her staff of four could barely keep up through the lunch rushes. The morning was pure chaos. I even jumped in a few times behind the counter. Macy had simply given me a harried glance and didn't say a damn thing.

I might not have her magical abilities, but I could pour a regular pressed coffee. I could refill the various milks and condiments. It was the least I could do since I usually mooched a table from her most days. I wasn't used to being bored. I hated it.

Gage usually kept me occupied most of the time. Both of us researching baby stuff, going to a few appointments.

Sex.

Lord, the sex. We kept trying to get to know one another, but then he'd laugh at something I said, and he'd invariably lean in to kiss me and then there went the research. And our clothes.

Mostly our clothes.

The weeks had been a blur of baby stress and Gage's inventive sleepwalking traps.

My new doctor didn't know a whole lot about sleepwalking, but she was researching it. She'd advised a follow-up visit to discuss her findings and an ultrasound in the coming weeks.

All in all, we were finding our footing. The days were getting longer and warmer. I'd showed him a few of my favorite spots on Main Street and we were finding new places to explore together. Both of us were starting over. It was like dating, only things felt a little bigger and a lot more claustrophobic. When I got too overwhelmed, I still had the tendency to push him away.

That was how I ended up in the coffee shop half the day.

Lately, he'd been a little preoccupied during the day. Always on his phone.

Sometimes he shared emails from his agent, who was forever trying to woo Gage back to the racetrack.

I hated that my stomach got knotted up the minute he put his hands on his phone. Eventually, he'd have to figure out a way to change careers. Or he'd simply fall in line. How many times could Harry call him or text him before Gage simply said yes?

"Moose!"

I looked up from the paper I was *not* looking at.

Ellie and Jodi called out the happy sing-song name. And right on cue, our favorite afternoon shy guy filled the doorway. Large shoulders blocked the watery sunshine spilling into the café. He averted his gaze before lifting his head.

Though he wasn't the most sociable dude, he had a way of looking at a woman as if she was the center of his universe.

Especially when it came to Vee.

"Hi, ladies." Moose—also known as Murphy Masterson—was a regular. Almost everyone was in a town as small as Crescent Cove, but Moose came in every day without fail at one in the afternoon. Right after the main lunch rush, but before the teens got out of school and took over my reading area for schoolwork and gossip.

I might need to bring my cup up to the counter for no reason whatsoever.

Except maybe to make fun of Vee when she caught sight of Moose.

I shifted to the side of the counter.

Vee came out of the back where she made her crazy confections. She smoothed her brightly colored braid, toying with the tail as she got to the register. She changed her hair like I changed my underwear. Today, it was done in pink and purple streaks. "Hi, Murphy."

"Miss Veronica."

I resisted the urge to lean on the side counter with heart eyes. They were so danged cute.

Yes, there was no shortage of romance around me, and shockingly, I actually felt charmed by it. Maybe because my own romance was going surprisingly well.

Legos, unplanned babies, peanut butter, and all.

"You're going to grow out of that corner."

I grinned over my shoulder at Macy. "It's Moose time."

She tucked her towel into her apron. "They should just fuck already."

I snorted. "Two shy people? Come on, we need more fairy dust than that."

"Vee is the least shy person I know."

"Yeah, when it comes to us. Guys? Especially that guy? Talk about buttoned down."

"Hmm."

We both watched as Vee, normally smooth and skilled behind the counter, fumbled with Moose's repeat customer card. Their fingers brushed, and Moose's neck heated up like a burner on high. If either of them averted their eyes any more, they'd literally be on the floor.

Moose lifted his cup in thanks, disappointment flickering in his gaze when Vee was already rushing back into the kitchen.

"You'd think she was thirteen, not twenty-six when he was around," Macy muttered.

Considering I knew a little how that felt, I couldn't say a damn thing.

Macy wasn't through. "Don't see me blushing and fluttering around a male, now do you?"

John Gideon hadn't been in lately. I had it on good authority from Vee that he was Macy's brand of kryptonite. Something about his giant tool belt.

I'd just leave that line of conversation for another day.

I cleared my throat. "So, I'm bored as hell. Do you have anything you need me to help out with? You know, busy work?"

"You keep helping out, I'm going to have to put you on the roster, mocha."

"Would that be so bad?"

Macy folded her arms over her chest, a malevolent version of *It's the Great Pumpkin, Charlie Brown* peeking over her stacked arms from her T-shirt. "You angling for a job?"

I shrugged. I wanted more than that, but it was probably the first avenue I should try. "I could help out when you needed it."

"I'm kind of an asshole boss. I mean, we're friends-ish."

I laughed. "Ish."

She shrugged. "Whatever. If you don't care that I'm grouchy by nature, you can try it out. I don't want you crying to me when I snap at you because you do something I hate."

"That's different from how you already talk to me how?"

Macy just grunted. "Your funeral." She headed back to the main counter now that the heart eyes were brushed away. "You can mess with the displays you're always crying about."

I grinned. "Really?" I called after her.

She waved over her head. "Just do it already. I'm sick of hearing you whine about it."

I rushed back to my iPad and papers, shoving them back into my messenger bag. I debated running my bag upstairs, then decided I needed to change into clothes a little more suited for crawling around the floor rearranging mugs and memorabilia.

Just as I slung my bag over my shoulder, Gage came in the front door laughing with a stunning redhead and his brother. The strap fell off my shoulder as the bombshell woman in leather grabbed Gage and leaped onto his back.

"You will not cheap out on the shearing machine. I know a guy." She hopped down when she spotted me staring at them. "That hot piece has to be your girl." She punched Gage much like I usually did when he said something boneheaded.

Gage laughed and crossed to me. "Hey, huntress." He dropped a kiss on my shocked mouth. "Sorry. One of my favorite people came to town. I told you about Tish? The one who kept dodging my texts?"

I couldn't keep all of Gage's people straight from his racing days. Perhaps I would have paid attention a little more if I caught her name. "You mentioned someone named Burns, maybe?" My eyes cut to the pinup-worthy woman, then back to Gage.

"That's me, Tish Burns. Depends on how many beers deep we are which name he calls me." Tish sashayed up to me, her full hips swinging. She held her hand out to me, I took it and wasn't surprised to find her grip strong and sure.

Thankfully, she didn't try to rush up to me with a hug. I wasn't entirely sure I could stop myself from kicking her in the ankles. Maybe she'd topple on those platform heels.

Gage hauled me closer, his hand firmly tucked into my back pocket—his favorite place lately.

Well, second favorite place.

"She's here to help me gang up on Dare."

"I'd like to gang up on the Kramer boys, but alas, it's not meant to be." Tish's attention strayed to the counter. "What is that delicious scent?"

"Who knows. Macy—the owner of this place—has some sort of hoodoo voodoo when it comes to coffee. She won't tell me what she puts in mine."

Tish's eyebrow spiked. "In my world, that's called a roofie, babe."

Gage laughed and my need for violence grew. Was she an ex-girlfriend? "We call it magic. If she likes you, she won't take your coffee order, she'll just put it in front of you."

Tish let out a dubious grunt. "We'll just see about that."

Dare sighed. "Hey, Ry. I'll go make sure she doesn't make Jodi cry."

"Good idea." Gage grinned down at me before he tilted his head. "Everything okay?"

"Sure." I gave him a bright smile.

He shifted me in front of him, tucking his other hand in my remaining pocket. "I'm not sure I believe you."

I tried to wiggle away, but he held me fast. "I have to get upstairs."

"Oh. I was hoping you'd have lunch with us."

"I already ate." The snarky tone to my voice made me want to saw off my tongue.

"Okay." He extended the word and I really knew my bitch voice was in use.

I smoothed my finger down his button-down shirt. He'd definitely gotten dressed with a little more care that morning. "I kinda am working for Macy now."

"Kinda? That's great." His face cleared, and he hugged me. "I knew you would talk to her."

"Don't get all excited. I'm just feeling her out. A little part time action to start."

"Well, come over to talk to us when you're back."

I slipped away with a nod, grabbed my bag, and rushed over to the side doors to the apartment access. And okay, maybe I took a little more time with my hair and makeup than I usually did.

However, I now had another pair of jeans to add to the nope pile.

I sighed and tugged on a pair of black pants that were becoming a staple of my life. They were far more forgiving. I stepped into ballet flats and swapped out my T-shirt for a longer one that would cover my growing bump.

By the time I got back downstairs, Dare, Gage and Tish were laughing at a table. Vee's now famous bagel chips were being dunked in soup as Tish kept testing out every other plate but her own.

"Hey, there you are." Gage waved me over. "You gotta see this."

There wasn't a chair for me, but he didn't seem to care. He hooked his arm around my waist and dumped me on his lap. Not sure why he thought I was his personal rag doll. And I tried not to love it every single damn time.

He held his cell so I could see it. "Listen to this from Harry. 'The Tide people want you, for fuck's sake. Pick up the damn phone.'" Gage shook his head. "Not only that, but they want me to do commercials."

Tish laughed. "Covered in grease and," she snapped her fingers, "look at how white!"

Dare just shook his head. "My brother in commercials."

I blinked and my gaze jerked to Gage's face. "Tide? Isn't that a big deal?"

Gage shrugged. "They tried to get me before, but I was tied up with my last sponsor. Their promotional schedule is ridiculous. I'd never leave my old trailer."

"That's for damn sure." Dare grunted. "You'd barely get to drive with their program." He took a bite of his club sandwich.

I played with the soft hair at the nape of Gage's neck. Just as I was getting used to him being around everything was shifting. I tried to smile as they talked about race schedule things I didn't understand. The entire time, Gage kept fiddling with the hem of my shirt. Little absent brushes that made me want to push him away.

Luckily, Macy came by with her trusty bussing tray. "How is everything?"

Tish sat back in her chair. "If you don't tell me what's in this coffee, I'm going to—"

"What? Not come back? Good luck with that, cayenne."

Tish blew out raspberries. "Nothing but haterade out of you."

Man, evidently Macy liked Tish a lot. She already had a nickname. Too bad Tish didn't know Macy's nicknames usually included a bit of a clue on the ingredients to their particular blend of coffee. Then again, there was always something to her coffee that the proprietress would never fess up to. Even a few purported "supertasters" couldn't figure out what was in her drinks.

Another of the angles I wanted to talk to Macy about. To play up her special blends—both drinks and popcorn. I bet I could sell her popcorn on a website. I figured my kid would come out looking like a peanut covered in cheddar and caramel with how much I ate the stuff. Either that or my kid would never eat it.

"I hear you and Ry are talking about working together."

Macy glanced at me, then Gage. "Yeah, I'm going to use her and abuse her. Hope you don't mind."

"She's got tons of ideas. Wait until you hear about the movie—"

I tugged on his hair and he stopped talking. He shot me a look. "Gage talks too much."

"What about movies?" Macy asked absently as she cleared the table.

I swallowed down my nerves. "I'll tell you later."

Macy paused and gave me one of her hard looks. In true Macy fashion, she didn't say a thing. Just finished her job and gave a halfhearted smile before she headed back to the main counter.

"Friendly, isn't she?" Tish quipped.

"One of the few people on this fucking street who doesn't talk a body to death." Dare filched the last bagel chip from Gage's plate.

Gage tightened his hold on my hip when I tried to stand up. "Why did you stop me?"

"Because I haven't even worked with her for a day yet. Maybe I could ease into the subject of *my* ideas for *her* business." This time, I did break away. "Speaking of. If I want to actually have a paycheck, I should go over there and get to work." He frowned but let me go. "Have fun with your lunch."

My belly was jangling with all the new information and the raucous laughter coming from their table. Even Dare seemed amused by Tish. The woman who could effortlessly talk to both of them about car things. All of the things I would never be able to do. Partly because I didn't care, to be honest.

But it also wasn't really in my wheelhouse. Since I'd moved to Crescent Cove, I barely drove my car. Everything was in walking distance. And as spring started crawling out of the rainy season, it made even less sense to drive anywhere unless I had to go to one of the surrounding towns. When that happened, I was usually with Gage.

Or at least I had been. Would that change now?

Gage waved before he left with his crew. I'd gotten used to his undivided attention, and I wasn't wild about the niggle of unease mixed with jealousy. As if my brain wasn't clogged with enough to worry about now, I had to deal with that?

Calm the hell down, Ry, and do your job.

I settled in with the newest shipments of Macy's merchandise and spent the next few hours redoing her grid layout. Macy came by a few times to make a comment, but generally, she left me alone. I was in the middle of a television display on one of the shelves when I had to jump in and help with the dinner rush.

I wished desperately for coffee but forged on with a large ginger-lime flavored water concoction that Macy set next to me around seven o'clock.

"You've been at it for hours." Vee settled on the floor next to me with another water. "I love that new table you did out front. I asked Macy if I could switch out the window graphic next weekend." She breathed out a happy sigh. "Spring is in the air."

"I found a box full of pretty spring cups for teas and flavored waters." I dug behind me and pulled out a soft pink and green frosted cup that was unreasonably tall but seemed to fly off the shelves. "Maybe something with these colors?"

"Oh." She snatched it out of my hand. "Maybe some baby-friendly drinks to lure all the preggers girls in."

"Smart." I took back the cup. "I didn't know you did all that. I mean, I've seen you do the menu board, but the windows are crazy."

Vee shrugged. "I went to art school, but couldn't decide between baking or art. Then I met Macy and got to do both."

"It's got to be amazing to be good at something." I picked through the cups and started organizing them by color.

"What, like you and this?" She waved her arm around the three different tables and half wall of cubbies I'd arranged.

I waved her off. "That's just making things look cute."

"Macy can build the hell out of nineteen drink orders in less than a minute each. However, her idea of decorating is adding a bat or skull."

"Hey, I like her aesthetic."

Vee linked her arms around her knees and rocked a little. "It works, but this is amazing, Ry. Really." She reached over and touched my belly. "And you're cooking that little nugget too."

At her wistful sigh I tilted my head. "Thanks. Cooking the baby isn't exactly tough. Luckily for me, I don't really have the nausea thing too often." Nope, I just had the super sleepwalking thing, but I didn't need to get into that with her.

"What's it feel like?"

"Like my jeans don't fit and I want all the salt." I laughed. "Why?"

She shrugged. "I always wanted a bunch of kids. And here I am. I can't even keep a boyfriend around long enough to get him suited up, let alone convince him about forever."

"Really? You're gorgeous. You should have guys knocking down my displays to get to you."

"Thanks. I'm too weird, I guess. And I don't know what to say to guys."

"Like Moose?"

She blushed. "He's sweet. I'm just getting impatient, I guess."

"You're only what? Twenty-six, I think Macy said."

She nodded. "That biological clock is ticking away."

"You've got plenty of time."

"You're the same age, aren't you?"

A little younger, but I didn't think I should mention that. "Yeah, I guess I am."

She rolled to her feet and brushed off her butt. "See? I'm way behind."

"Ugh, enough with the baby talk. You're killing me," Macy called from the front counter. "Hey, Ry, want to watch a movie after we're done, or do you have something going with the boyfriend?"

Was that what I'd call Gage? My boyfriend?

I supposed it was less crass than baby daddy. I was tired of all the baby talk myself and I was the one carrying one.

"I'll text him. I'm feeling a little like *The Texas Chainsaw Massacre*."

"God, yes."

I laughed and we started the closing process for the café. It felt good to be a productive part of a team. I didn't even know how much I'd missed it until I got it back. The chattering girls, Macy pretending to be grouchy, even Vee's incessant baby questions had my mood brightening.

I texted Gage about hanging out with Macy and received three follow-up texts from him to get me to ask Macy about my ideas. He was relentless, but the little bubble of warmth was spreading.

Finally, me and Macy collapsed onto the couch with a bowl of popcorn—a new Cajun concoction with a toffee base. Honestly, the girl was going to make me weigh five-hundred pounds by the end of this pregnancy.

I groaned as I took another handful. "You know, you really need to sell this. I bet it would fly off the shelves as fast as the coffee. Hell, it would probably get people buying more drinks."

Macy gave me one of her half-grins and took her own handful. "Is this one of your ideas?"

I choked and reached for my water. When I stopped coughing, I gave her a weak smile. "What? No." Maybe. Yes. So much yes.

"Mmm-hmm."

I sighed. "Gage is such a big mouth."

"He means well. Mostly. He's definitely the pushier of the Kramer brothers. Then again, Kelsey ended up moved in with Dare before she could even blink, so maybe not."

"They are very pushy and bossy."

And yummy, though I wouldn't say that aloud. Probably. Though Gage was far yummier.

"Good thing they're hot. And evidently, they wield their dumbstick with a powerful breeding sense." She shuddered and inched down into a comfortable position.

I laughed and relaxed. "Truth."

"So, tell me your ideas, girl."

I nibbled on my lip. "I don't want to overstep."

"Like I have trouble telling you when you are?"

"That is very true." I angled myself toward her. "I was thinking maybe we should actually have movie nights and set up some couches and recliners, maybe? Sell your crazy-delicious popcorn and give people something to do at night. It's so dead in the Cove after seven o'clock, for God's sake. It's an untapped moneymaker."

When she didn't shoot down the idea, I rushed on and gave her some details from my research about showing movies. What we could and couldn't do with trademarking and licensing.

Three hours later, we'd never started the movie, but we did have a plan.

One that I'd mostly come up with. How about that?

Maybe the idea of Rylee Ford being a businesswoman wasn't so insane after all.

TWENTY

I GRINNED AT THE TEXTS FROM RYLEE. "FINALLY."

Dare rested his beer against his belt. "Finally, what?"

"Ry has been in nightly pow-wow sessions with Macy about her ideas for the café. She's been so hesitant to share them all. She's perfect for the damn job. I just wish she believed it."

Dare's eyebrows rose.

"What?"

"You're really all in with this girl, huh?"

"This girl? She's your sister-in-law too, bro."

"Oh, I know. Not that we ever really saw Rylee until recently. The sisters aren't exactly close these days. Though they are bonding through babies now." He shook his head. "How that fucking happened, man, I do not know."

"Well, if you didn't get the birds and bees memo, I'm sure Pops would love to give you a refresher."

Dare almost spit out his beer. He finished swallowing. "Pass."

The familiar scent of motor oil and gasoline settled me. I kicked out my legs as I leaned against the vintage Chevy Dare was working on. "I was thinking about using that old VW Bug shell in the junkyard to make a couch for Rylee."

Dare set his beer down. "Is that right?"

"Yeah, she's got this movie night idea for Brewed Awakening. I thought if they had fun couches for people to sit on, it might get people even more excited about coming in."

"What about that Tide sponsor offer?"

I stood up straight and swapped out my empty for a bottle of water. I had my girl to watch out for tonight. Dare glanced at my drink choice, but in usual Dare form, he didn't comment. He did look a little surprised, which made me take a longer pull from the plastic bottle. Someday maybe my brother would believe that I wasn't the partying kid he remembered from our mutual racing days anymore.

"What about it?" I asked.

"Seems pretty amazing. Their driver stalling out on a drug test is a damn shame, but it could be good for you."

"I told you I'm retired." I gestured toward the back of the garage. "Tish has been here talking about the space all fucking day, man. I'm not going back on the road. I want this."

"For now."

I drained the water and paced the area between the cars. "Not sure how many times I need to explain this to you. I want this garage. I want us to make a go of this together."

I'd tried being subtle with my brother. Then I'd tried spelling it all out. He was obtuse, regardless.

"And I'm not exactly Mr. Moneybags like you are." Dare threw his rag down on the engine block he was cleaning. "What the hell do I have to bring to the party? Have you thought of that?"

"Expertise? You still have connections in the network."

"Ah, enough with that shit. I've been out of the game so long that I'm a fossil."

"I don't think you understand just how legendary you were in the pit." I shot my bottle into the recycle bin. "I've always been Dare's little brother. Good with an engine and an idea, but innovative? Nope. Not like you."

"Bullshit."

"You're a genius at pulling engines apart. I have ideas coming out my ass about redoing cars so they're cool as fuck, but I don't want to find some other engine expert. I want you. Between you, our men, and Tish, we could make this garage into something amazing. I have friends who blow money on cars all the time. Imagine what we could make for them?"

Dare leaned under the hood of the '67 Chevy. "So you can get me all in and then you'll go take a job with Tide or Exxon or whomever comes looking for you with an amazing deal in a few months? What am I supposed to do after that?"

I crossed the garage and turned him to face me. "I'm not going any-fucking-where. I want this." I waved my hand toward the old garage that had so much space and great bones. I could see what it could be with some time and restoration already. Just like the cars we would work on. Together. "I want Rylee and the baby. I want a damn family again. I'm tired of being alone out there."

I'd shouted it. I didn't even realize just how pissed off I was at being underestimated time and again until I'd said it.

"I've been gone for years, man. And yeah, I've got the money to start this up, but without you, it wouldn't get anywhere close to what it could be. You've been hiding under oil changes and air filters for too long, bro. You know you're bored. You want this as much as I do."

Dare's jaw clenched and his hands fisted at his sides.

"Am I wrong?"

"It's not just about what I want. It never has been."

"Well, it's time to take something for you. Sure, it might not work, but what if it does? You and your family would be set, and you'd actually enjoy what you're doing again. You've been smiling all night since you've had your grease monkey paws all over that Chevy block."

"Fuck off." Dare pushed away from me and picked up his beer again.

"What, are you going to go to the next town over and find another job where you're working with a bunch of punk kids who don't know the difference between a Ford and a Hyundai?"

He finished his beer and shot the bottle into the recycling bin so hard the bottle shattered. "Dammit."

"Dare, we can do this. I already went to the bank with my business plan."

"What?" He turned started eyes on me.

"Yeah. I'm serious about this. It's not just an idea. I've been researching machines. For fuck's sake, I bought a house." My voice exploded.

"Where?"

"On the lake. A big house that I can grow into with Rylee."

"Does she know this?"

"I'm trying like hell to convince her, man. Or I will be soon. I'm not sure what I have to do to convince you people that I'm not going any-damn-where. I'm home, man. I want Crescent Cove to be where I raise my kids. I want my little girl or boy to grow up with his cousins and make friends. I want him safe, here in this small freaking town."

Dare's winter blue eyes were wide and for the first time, doubt wasn't hanging over his damn head. "You're serious."

I stalked away from him. "Would you like a kidney? The deed to my new house to prove it? What do you fucking need?"

Dare was silent. He took a bottle of water from the cooler and moved back to the car.

The silence stretched for damn near five minutes before he spoke again.

"I have some conditions."

I tipped my head back, my throat clogging with emotion. "Yeah, like what?"

"We don't just do the specialty cars. We gotta take care of the town too."

I groaned. "So boring."

"You say you want the small-town life. Well, guess what? Small town is affordable cars that need to be serviced too. Once JT's is closed, people won't have a place to go. Except for the corporate rip-off places. I won't stand for that."

I sighed and nodded. "You've got a point."

"If we're doing this, we gotta take care of our own."

Dare's face was impassive as he stood beside the car. My

responsible, stable brother had a point. I was so set on the future, on the fun, that I didn't think about the responsible side of things. Things I still needed to learn, evidently.

And about the people who owned the cars. People were always most important.

"You have to tell Tish about that part."

Dare grunted. "You're still a punk."

I grinned. "Yeah, well, I didn't say I'd totally changed." I crossed to him and dragged him in for a hard hug. "Hot damn, we're doing this."

Dare hugged me back with a hearty slap. "I guess we are."

"Wait till I tell Ry. She's going to flip." I dug out my phone to text her that I had big news. I paused. "Maybe a surprise is in order."

"You sure about that? In my experience, girls really aren't a big fan of surprises."

"This is a good surprise."

"Famous last words."

TWENTY-ONE

I HAD NO PRACTICE AT SETTING UP A ROMANTIC DINNER.

And a romantic dinner with a big news chaser, since Gage had said he had something important to share?

Yeah, I definitely had no idea there.

You'd figure after a couple of weeks of dating and basically living together—talk about putting the cart after the pregnant horse, but Gage and I were trying to make up for lost time—that I'd feel better about making a meal he might enjoy. But nope, I still felt as if I was mostly flying blind.

At least I wasn't entirely clueless. Most men tended to enjoy manly meats as a rule. Kel had said when she wanted to celebrate something with Dare or lure him into sex, she made him pot roast and green beans with mashed potatoes. I wasn't sure how that was a sex-conducive supper—I thought oysters were aphrodisiacs, not potatoes—but my sister had bagged herself the first Kramer man. She had to be wiser about such things than I was.

I flapped the plastic tablecloth I'd picked up at the thrift store over my small circular kitchen table and coughed at the dust. Homemaker of the year, I was not. I was going for quaint dinner atmosphere, not high society.

Good thing too, since my budget didn't extend to such extravagances. The secondhand store served my shopping needs just fine right now. They even had baby stuff. I'd started buying a few things here and then and tucking them away in the hall closet. A package of unused blankets. A package of brand-new sippy cups. And on the last trip, a bright pink elephant with a plaid trunk.

Not that I was hoping for a girl or anything.

So, yes, I totally was.

I still felt strange shopping for baby things, and not just because I'd only made it through the first few chapters of my new pregnancy book. I just couldn't believe it was all really happening. Even after confirmation from the doctor that sperm indeed had met egg and all systems were go, I couldn't help doubting that it could be true. I hadn't had many physical changes yet. Those unfortunate fainting episodes, my jeans getting shoved to the back of the closet, some definite exhaustion, and that bout of throwing up that day with Gage all counted in the symptoms column. Still, nothing that screamed knocked up.

Well, other than how hard I was hitting the peanut butter. But I did that sometimes during PMS.

So much for neon signs. This preggo deal was stealthy sometimes.

Or maybe I still kept figuring someone would take away this little slice of happiness I'd stolen for myself.

I brought over the fat candlestick I'd also gotten secondhand and plopped it in the center of my table. Around it I placed a twisted sprig of flowers I'd, ahem, borrowed from one of Macy's countertop displays. She'd had plenty.

The timer dinged and I hurried to take out my roast. I pulled it out of the oven and wrinkled my nose as I looked it over. Seemed a little overdone. Dry? I'd just call it charbroiled.

Macy had already taught me that in retail, how you presented things and the language you used made a difference. I'd picked up some of that stuff from my various jobs over the years, but Macy was running through the basics with me. As if we might just be partners someday.

Another thing I was afraid to hope for.

The carrots along the sides of my roast seemed pretty good though. I popped one in my mouth to test it and let out a little moan at the burst of honey sweetness from the glaze I'd used.

Cooking was never going to be a huge skill of mine, but maybe I could keep me and the kid alive while Gage was on the road without resorting to microwave everything.

Just microwave most things. And she'd be on pureed bananas most of the time for a while anyway.

There, see, I could think of Gage being gone as if it was any old thing. Just normal life.

Because I was certain that was his big news tonight. He'd given me a heads up with that email he'd received. He couldn't pass up an offer to join a huge team. Why should he? Just to play house with the chick he'd accidentally impregnated?

Okay, so I was beginning to believe we were far more than that. Deep down, I was having feelings for him that weren't the friends with benefits kind.

Ah, hell, who was I kidding? I was more than halfway gone for the guy.

That little quarter of an inch left around my heart was purely self-protective barbed wire. If I went all in, let's just say I wouldn't be able to blithely make him going away charbroiled pot roast dinners.

As it was, I might've been sniffling a bit that didn't have a thing to do with the puff of smoke that came out of my roast when I carved it open.

Betty Crocker I was not.

I slid it onto the platter thingy I'd borrowed from my sister and garnished it with a few of the carrots—the ones that didn't end up in my mouth. I shifted to finish up my potatoes and served them and my honey-glazed green beans just as the door opened.

"Honey, I'm home," Gage called.

I laughed and sniffled a little more. Stupid smoke.

"Oh, you cooked? For real?"

"What gave it away? The apron?" I looked down at myself and

grinned at the phrase about tongue-kissing the cook. That had also been a thrift store find. I'd probably better stay out of there for a while.

"Also, the delicious smells. What did you make? Oh." He stopped halfway over to me and stared at the table. "You did all this?"

"You said it was a big night." I shrugged. "So, I figured I'd play at being the little wifey—um, I mean woman."

There was no missing how Gage's gaze sharpened. His caramel brown eyes raked over me and for a second, I wanted to snatch the word back.

I wasn't greedy enough to assume more than I had already was on the table. Not when he'd already given me so much more than I'd ever expected.

"It all looks wonderful." He moved to me and cupped my shoulders as he pressed a kiss to my forehead. Then he gripped my chin and took possession of my mouth, slipping his tongue inside to toy with mine. How he could be so sweet and so commanding at the same time, I would never understand.

At least not when I was pooled on the kitchen floor.

"The roast is burnt," I gasped once he eased back.

"Put more gravy on it," he suggested before he headed toward the bathroom.

Huh. That was a good idea.

I'd just finished ladling the gravy over the roast and the potatoes when he reemerged. "Oh, crap, I forgot dessert."

He licked his lips, eyeing me thoroughly. Under my apron and T-shirt, my nipples hardened to points. Didn't take much lately, and Gage's smolder worked like magic. "I think we can make do."

"Celebration nookie?"

"You could say that. Or just anytime nookie. Or Gage-can't-keep-his-hands-off-Rylee-because-she's-so-fucking-gorgeous-he-can't-breathe-nookie."

I smiled and poked at the roast on the platter with my long-handled fork. Also borrowed from my sister. "You're a sure thing. You don't have to flatter me, Kramer."

"Who's flattering? I'm just telling the truth." He came close and tugged me against him. "How do you feel about eating dinner while sitting on my lap?"

"I feel like that's an exercise that has a limited time engagement." I patted my belly and looked up under my lashes to find him doing that molten gaze thing again.

"All the more reason we should do it now." He sat down and started to drag me to him, but I held him off, giggling and darting out of his reach.

Since I had a good idea of what his news involved, it was better if I kept my distance. I had rehearsed my speech, and if he was too close, I might not be able to pull it off.

If I even could at all.

"Ruiner." But he smiled at me just the same as I sat down opposite him at the table.

"I don't want to interfere with your digestion. Supper is the most important meal of the day."

"I thought it was breakfast?"

"Yeah, but when are we ever up early enough to eat before lunchtime?"

"Oh, I'm up." He grinned.

I rose and tossed a cloth napkin at him. I'd forgotten to add those to my dinner spread. Utensils too, which I removed from the drawer beside the stove. "You're definitely up, but we aren't worried about food before lunchtime. How's that?"

"We have other priorities, what can I say?"

"Uh-huh." I sat back down and dug in.

"Wow, this all looks great." Gage cut off a piece of the roast and slid it through the pool of gravy on his plate. His face as he chewed and swallowed was fairly priceless. "Tastes it too."

Since I'd just taken my first bite too, I had to laugh and wipe my mouth with my napkin. "Maiden voyage. Next time, if it comes out this way, we'll just order pizza."

"We do get a family discount from the best place around."

So silly how even the words family discount made a nice little glow take root in my chest. "We do."

"The potatoes are delicious though. And the green beans. You got more carrots than I did."

I wrapped my arm around my plate as I continued to fork up veggies and he laughed.

"Guess you need them more, since you've barely gained an ounce yet."

"Tell that to my ass."

"Oh, I will. I'm hoping to see it up close and personal again soon."

The man made it very hard to stay guarded.

And fully clothed.

We ate companionably as we talked about our days. Me working with Macy and learning more about what it was like to be on the opposite side of the counter at Brewed Awakening. Gage working with his brother and enjoying seeing what kinds of different cars came into the shop. He was talking about a sweet cherry red Chevelle he'd done some maintenance on when I finished my last bite of pot roast and let 'er rip.

"It's all right, you know."

Gage poured more gravy on the last of the potatoes. He'd really seemed to like them, which helped to make up for the fail whale of my pot roast. "It was really good. Just the potatoes are my favorite part—"

"Not dinner." I gripped my napkin and tried to remember my speech. Somehow I'd forgotten how to start it off. "You can just say it. I promise I'm prepared."

He sat back in his chair. "Not so sure about that. It's a big leap."

"It is, and I want you to take it. You deserve it. After all the wins you racked up, you should have a big team behind you and a chance to be at the top of the points standings once again."

His mouth tightened. Instead of thanking me for my considerate response, he tilted his head. "You know about points standings?"

"I've been doing my research." All things told, it was more pleasant to read about hot racing dudes than it was to bone up on hemorrhoids, thickening mucus, and swollen ankles. "You were a pretty huge fish. What the hell are you doing here?"

"Did it ever occur to you I want to be here?"

"Yeah, because it was a lark. I get that. You were bored with the same old, same old, but this has a chance to be something different. You can notch a place in history."

"I already have a place in history, baby." The lazy way he said it should have annoyed me, not make my panties wet.

Pregnancy hormones were detrimental to me standing strong.

"Yes, but that's yesterday's news." I tried to pretend I didn't see how his brows beetled together. I knew that sounded bitchy, but couldn't he see that I was trying to be the bigger person here? "You know how quickly the public forgets you if you don't stay front and center. Do you really want to bypass an opportunity to be on top again? Possibly bigger than you've ever been before?"

He took his time answering me. So long that I knew whatever he had to say would be a doozy.

I was right.

"I had a buddy who didn't come back from a race one time. Car behind him clipped him and he bumped the car beside him and next thing any of us knew, he crashed into the wall." Gage's voice was hollow in a way I'd never heard before. "This was before any of the new security measures were put into place, but still. He had a kid. A wife. His whole life ahead of him."

I wanted to take it all back. *No. Don't go. Don't take the chance.*

Don't leave us.

A shiver went through me and I rubbed my forearms to ward it off. "There's new security measures, you just said it yourself. It's safer, isn't it?"

"Yes, it's safer. But there are no guarantees. And Jesus, Rylee, I have a kid on the way. Do you honestly think I want to be out there pushing my luck every day? Before, I didn't see it that way. Rarely thought about the danger at all. Now I can't help thinking of all I have at home." He pushed his hand through his hair. "I didn't understand why Dare quit. I didn't get it back then. Now I do."

Tears were constricting my throat and I wasn't sure if I could force the words out. "You're worried about us and I appreciate that so much. But if we hold you back from what we love, you're going to resent us eventually. You won't be able to help yourself."

"Don't you get it yet? I don't love racing anymore." He shoved his chair back from the table. "I love you, Rylee."

TWENTY-TWO

RYLEE STARED AT ME AS IF I'D JUST SHOCKED HER DOWN TO HER TOES.

Because she was the most stubborn woman I'd ever known, I probably had.

I rose from the chair I'd pushed back and walked to the sink. I didn't have far to go since her kitchen was the size of the bathroom in our new place.

My new place right now. But I still had hope.

I was stubborn too. Had to be to deal with Ry.

"Is this because I'm pregnant?" she asked finally.

I didn't turn to face her because I was afraid I wouldn't be rational. She tended to push all my buttons, and when I had my pants on, I didn't always appreciate it.

"You mean do I love you because you're carrying my child?"

"Don't make it sound so...intimate."

"It is intimate. Christ, woman. How does it get any more intimate than that?"

My beautiful pain in the ass didn't respond.

"No, I don't love you because you're pregnant. I love you because you're strong and smart and determined and I never know what you'll throw at me from one moment to the next. And I love you because you want our baby as much as I do. You want to be the best parent you can be even though you're scared shitless. Just as I am. And I love you because I'm clearly a little bit crazy." I huffed out a breath. "That cover it?"

She pushed to her feet and started clearing the table. I still didn't look at her, but I heard her doing it and it pissed me off. Then she slammed her platter on the wood. "We've only known each other since before Christmas. You can't possibly love me yet."

"No? Is there a date when it's allowed? Tell me and I'll pretend I don't until then if it suits you."

She surprised the hell out of me by laughing. "I'm trying to be reasonable."

"Why start now?"

I expected her to rail at me. Instead, she laughed again. "You're right. We haven't been reasonable from the fucking start."

"It's still better than me delivering you a pizza. That's only started like what, fifty pornos? And look at Dare and Kel. They're blissfully happy and don't give a crap what anyone thinks."

"That's the only dumb thing Kelsey's ever done though. Well, minus dating Tommy the loser, but that's over with. Me, I'm the queen of dumb moves. It's so not the same."

"You're going to have to tell me what's dumb about finding the love of your life and settling down and being happy. Because I'm not following."

"What if you're settling? If you're confusing hot chemistry and cute baby toes with a lifetime love? How can we possibly know so fast?"

"How does anyone know? There are no goddamn guarantees for anything on this planet, huntress, and especially not when it comes to finding the perfect person for you. Not someone who's perfect, period, but perfect for you. Huge difference."

"Super quick to say I'm not perfect, weren't you?"

"No love goggles here, babe."

I wasn't surprised when the balled-up cloth napkin hit me dead center in the back. I bent to pick it up and pitched it back at her. She grabbed it against her chest, screwing up her face until I was terrified she was going to cry.

But she surprised me one more time.

"I've always been jealous of my sister. Standard younger sibling story. And then she got knocked up by the pizza delivery dude, and that should be the stupidest thing ever and yet it turned into this grand love and she has everything. Absolutely everything." Rylee's chin wobbled. "There's no way the same could happen for me."

"You're right. If you shut it down before we even have a chance to see what happens, it won't happen. Not just for you, but me too. You'll be denying us both."

"You didn't mention the baby."

"The best gift we can give that kid is parents who love each other. But I won't pretend for the sake of my child. That does no one any good, especially the baby." I stepped forward and gripped her elbows, drawing her against me. "Luckily, I don't have to pretend a damn thing. I love you so much I can't think around it. Can't be smart or reasonable or—"

She rose up on her tiptoes and our mouths met as if we'd designed it just that way. God knows she wasn't quite tall enough to cover the distance if I hadn't lowered my head. But I was craving the honeyed sweetness of her mouth and the flash of her dark eyes before she closed them and gave herself over to me. Her heart slamming beat for beat against mine as we fought our way through the kiss. Until there was just heat and hunger and a bottomless well of love that didn't have a beginning and hopefully wouldn't have an end.

I let go of her elbows and she wrapped her arms around my neck, boosting herself up so that her legs wound around my waist. And wrenched her mouth away from mine.

"I love you too. I don't want you to leave. That makes me a shrew, I know, but I don't fucking care. I want to be selfish and keep you for myself. The rest of the world got their time with you. Now it's my chance and I'm taking it." She framed my face between her palms. "Please, stay with me. Stay with us. If I have to get three jobs if this thing with Macy doesn't work out, I will. I mean I have savings, but that only lasts so long. And if I get fired from two of them, I'll get two more. We can make it work."

For a second, I didn't reply. I probably didn't even breathe. That could've been why my head was throbbing as if I was at imminent risk of a cardiac event.

And this time, it wasn't even the head below my waist.

"Baby, I'm really fucking rich."

She pursed her lips. "Seriously? After that speech, that's what you lead off with?" She whacked me hard in the arm.

I grinned. "I didn't say that to brag, huntress. I was just saying you don't have to work if you don't want to. You can stay home with the baby for as long as you'd like, or not at all. You can do whatever you want with your life. I'm just asking to share it. That's all."

Her dark eyes filled, and she waved her hand in front of her face as if she was suddenly hot. "Hormones. Don't mind me. I'm not actually crying."

A tear plopped on my shirt. Then another. "And that's not actually liquid?"

"Don't make me hit you again when I'm trying to bask in your sweetness."

I took hold of one of her hands and brought it to my mouth, kissing her knuckles. "I bought us a house."

"What?"

"I bought us—"

"No, no, I heard the words, but they just didn't compute. How could you have bought us a house when you were leaving town to go back to racing until I just stopped you with my impassioned plea?"

I laughed so hard I nearly dropped her. "Huntress, I was never going back to racing. That was a story you came up with all your own."

"But the email—and you saying you had big news. I didn't make those things up. Oh. Oh. You meant the house." She pulled her hand free from my grip and pressed it to her mouth. "What if I don't like it?"

"There's room for a tent. There's about six acres give or take."

"Now I'm really going to hit you."

I grinned and turned to set her on the narrow countertop beside the stove. I would've preferred to put her on the kitchen table so I could live out one of my favorite sex fantasies but getting it on over the remains of an overcooked roast didn't quite measure up.

The counter could've worked as a fine substitute if it had been bigger than the span of my hand. But that was why I'd bought a house. We'd have many surfaces in our own place to desecrate.

And the kitchen counter was extremely spacious. Yes, I'd checked, and not so I could prepare our Thanksgiving turkey with room to spare.

"Oliver took me through it and it's big enough for us and the baby. I could build on a pole barn if I wanted to, which is kinda important considering what I have in mind job-wise. Plus, there's tons of yard for the kid or even kids if we decide to go there. It's not a starter place we'd have to upgrade in a couple years. It's move-in ready. And ready for someone to grow roots there. For us to grow roots there. If you love it like I do."

She bit her lower lip, dragging it between her teeth in that way that made me crazy. Especially since I'd already been fantasizing about her naked beside the Thanksgiving turkey.

Sort of.

"Why do you need a pole barn? What is a pole barn? Are there different kinds of barns?"

"Yeah, but we'll discuss that another time. Basically, so I can house cars there as necessary. In case I want or need to take my work home. I'm going into business with my brother. We're taking over the shop and we're going to not only keep the cars of Crescent Cove running smoothly, we're going to make kickass, specialized vintage cars. With all the racing people I know, there's so much we can do to help them spend their cash on a one of a kind Kramer custom car."

"You're going into business with Dare. Here in Crescent Cove. And you want to build a pole barn, at the house you're going to live at full time. With me and the baby."

"Yes. Assuming you don't move into that tent in the backyard."

"I'd still stop inside for conjugal visits."

"Well, of course."

"Especially during the second trimester. I'm not far into it yet, but holy crap. Just looking at you makes me want to pull off my pants right here."

I swallowed and focused in on her stretchy yoga pants with the little Mickey Mouse heads all over them. A little weird, but she was hot anyway. If I could get turned on by the thought of her beside a dressed bird, I could definitely handle her clad in mouse wear. "We should probably finish talking first, but I'm good with a break if you need one. Just for your benefit of course."

"Your altruism is truly commendable." Her throat rippled as she swallowed deeply. "How far away is this house? Since I just kinda found a sleep therapy group where a bunch of us freaks get together and talk out our issues. I've only gone once, just today, but I'm hopeful that maybe it'll help."

"You're not a freak." When she ducked her head, I tipped up her chin. "If you keep calling the woman I love names, I may have to shrink the size of your tent."

Her laughter was like music. Even better than the classic rock they played after I'd won a race and was standing in the winner's circle. "It's going to take some time for me to get there. But I'm trying. I'm really trying."

"I know you are. I can't ask for anything more."

"I can. Say the words."

"What words?" Then I smiled. "I love—"

"No, not that." She waved it off as if us loving each other was old news already. "Tell me you're staying with us. Me and the baby. Forever."

Somehow my smile even grew wider. "I'm staying." I tipped my forehead to hers. "Forever and a day."

She leaned up to brush her mouth over mine, her lips curving. "Now you can tell me you love me again."

"I love you, Rylee Ford." I kissed her softly. Sweetly. Then I moved down to lift up her shirt and pressed a kiss to the barely there swell of her belly. "I love you, baby Ford-Kramer."

Sooner rather than later, I intended to change that last name situation. But one day at a time.

I grinned against her stomach. With my huntress, one minute at a time was plenty.

She sniffled and ran her fingers through my hair, holding me in place. "I love you too. And I don't have confirmation yet, but I'm pretty sure she loves her daddy right back."

My chest tightened. "She?"

"C'mon, dude. You know you're going to be outnumbered in our house. It's practically a certainty."

Laughing, I stood up and gripped her hand between both of mine. "I can't wait."

EPILOGUE

"THIS FUCKER IS HEAVY." DARE GRUNTED AS HE LIFTED THE OPPOSITE end of the couch.

"You're the one who said it needed the reinforced frame." I might have underestimated the heft of the reclaimed VW Bug I'd made into a couch for Rylee's new venture with Macy at Brewed Awakening.

In the last month, she'd slowly brought Macy around to the idea of a movie corner as an addition to the business. My girl was a genius when it came to coming up with ideas to utilize the café for more than just the breakfast and lunch rush. Not that Macy really needed any help with foot traffic.

Macy put her hands on her hips. "When you said cool couch, that was not what I had in mind, Kramer."

It had been no easy feat to convince her to let me and Ry make some small changes to the far side of the café. I'd had to beg, cajole, and promise to do her oil changes for a year just to get her to let me bring in *one* couch.

But I knew after she saw the finished product, she'd want more. And Rylee would scream. I couldn't wait to see her face. Hopefully, that would soften her up for my other surprise.

I nodded to the side wall to my brother. "There before we drop this thing."

Dare only grunted again.

Macy rushed forward. "It's huge."

We set it down gently before Dare collapsed on the ruby red cushion. "That new frame Tish added made this a damn tank."

Macy popped her knuckles on one hand as she walked around the repurposed car. Me and Dare had made this first one into more of a loveseat size. The perfect way to get cozy, but keep it clean for the masses. If Rylee—and more importantly, Macy—liked the look, I had many more ideas for car couches. There were tons of different kinds that could be used inside and outdoors. The café had space to expand into the empty space next door.

Add a little patio on the back…

Well, the ideas were limitless. And I wasn't even the one coming up with them.

Rylee had been spinning ideas each night as we got ready for bed. Well, until I distracted her with her favorite nighttime snack. In the last few weeks, her sleepwalking had lessened. My Lego strategy helped for the nights when she got too wound up or stressed. It seemed that stress was the biggest amplifier for bouts of sleepwalking. Before a doctor's appointment or when she was gathering courage to talk to Macy about one of her plans were top of the list for causing her anxiety these days.

Luckily, I was bottom of the list lately.

We were having a good time playing house. She'd all but moved out of her apartment and into the house I'd bought for us, though she still kept the basics upstairs. I was pretty sure it was more for the huge bathroom than me, but I was making strides. My girl was independent as hell, but there were some days where she defaulted to stubborn for no other reason than making me insane.

I was learning that letting her come around to my ideas after planting a few seeds was better than demanding. Since I was used to snapping out orders to a team as their lead, that was taking some getting used to. That my brother and the love of my life required the same navigation was a mind-fuck too. But wonder of all wonders, Dare and I were getting along as well.

The three of us had decided to make it an even partnership. And so, *Kramer & Burns Garage* had been born. We'd originally wanted just cars, but with Tish as part of our group, we ended up with quite a few motorcycles looking for custom work too. We already had a waiting list for that aspect of the business. Even I hadn't believed things would move that fast.

Tish had put the word out and things sort of blew up from there.

Add in the racers I knew, and Dare's legendary engine expertise, and we'd had to actually hire someone to take care of the books and phones for us. That Lane happened to be a website wiz as well had all of us sighing with relief.

Well, until he started bugging us endlessly for pictures and videos for the garage's YouTube and social media platforms.

I'd had to tackle him before he could put a picture of the VW Bug sofa on our damn Instagram. After it was installed, and I surprised my girl, then he could do whatever the hell he wanted. Until then, he needed to cool it.

Damn, it was hard to keep a freaking secret in this town.

I just had one more to keep. And it was a burning a hole in my pocket.

The three of us took a step back to look at the car-couch against the wall. Macy was far too silent for my liking.

"Dad!" Wes, my nephew, came tearing into the café.

Dare looked over his shoulder. "Hey, bud. Where's your mom?"

"Can I see it now?" Wes plowed into me. Christ, he was getting big. I made room for him between me and his father.

Dare's eyebrow arched. "Where's your mom?"

Wes sighed dramatically. "She's sitting with Aunt Sage and Aunt Rylee upstairs."

"God, what are they hatching now?" I ruffled Wes's hair. "Isn't it cool?"

"So cool. Can I sit on it?"

I glanced at Dare then nodded. "Sure."

He dove onto it and bounced to the end where the polished headlight could be reached. "Does the light really work?"

"Sure does. Hit that button at the top. Right behind the cup holder."

He knelt on the seat to reach and punched the button. Then scrambled down in front of it. "Holy crap."

Instead of a regular headlight, we'd replaced it with an LED light that changed colors.

"Hey," Dare said sternly.

"Sorry. I mean, wow." Wes gave his dad a bit of side-eye then shifted toward the other headlight, which was also on. "This is so cool."

"Think your aunt Ry will think so?" I asked.

"Yeah, definitely." He came to stand between me and Dare again, mimicking his father's wide-legged stance and crossed arms.

I resisted the urge to snort. Would my kid mimic my mannerisms like that? Or would he or she be more like Ry? I couldn't wait to find out.

I nudged Macy. "What's the verdict?"

"It's pretty cool."

"To—"

"If you say I told you so, I'll rip your tongue out and use it for a gum scraper."

I pressed my lips together. That was Macy, ever full of sweetness and light. I cleared my throat. "Hey, Wes? Think you can go get your aunt Ry for me?"

"Yeah, sure." He tore off just as quickly as he'd come in.

Dare just shook his head. "All right, enough patting ourselves on the back. I got a GTO engine block to clean."

"The fun never ends."

Dare grinned. "Nope."

I laughed. Not sure I'd ever seen my brother so happy. I'd known he needed more than doing maintenance jobs on cars to fulfill that grease monkey heart of his. Now spending fourteen hours on an engine block made him bitch and moan, but there was always a sparkle of glee under the grumbles.

Dare gave Macy a salute, then headed out the front doors toward our garage.

"Did you make the special mix for me?"

Macy rolled her eyes at me. "Relax, Romeo. I got you covered."

I rubbed my palms against my jeans. "I'll relax after she says yes."

She shook her head. "This freaking town says yes all the time. Ankles to the sky without a thought to the consequences of the weird winds and water combo here. A little pixie dust and a glass of preggo water and you people are popping out kids freaking everywhere."

"I meant to marrying me."

"Oh. Well, yeah, that too. You just put the cart before the horse en masse."

"Sometimes that's the way it works. Doesn't mean I love her any less."

She huffed out something resembling a grumble and a grunt that would make Statler and Waldorf proud. Maybe one day she and Dare could dress up as them for Halloween. I was pretty sure Macy already had the old dudes from the Muppets on a shirt. She seemed to have an unending supply of rude shirts.

"I'll be right back with your special blend."

"Thanks, Mace."

"Yeah, yeah." She waved me off and headed back to the main counter.

"I'm coming."

My hands instantly itched at her voice. I turned toward Rylee in the doorway of the entrance to the café from the apartments. Wes was at her side, his cheek pressed to her growing belly. She smiled down at him and tucked his overlong wheat-colored hair behind his ear. "Now what's the surprise?"

"You gotta close your eyes."

Rylee closed her eyes good-naturedly. "Okay. Lead the way."

Wes carefully led her around the chairs to where I was standing. I winked at Wes and he laughed, then took off back toward the apartments.

"Wes?"

I moved in front of her, immediately cupping her little belly with one hand, then her face with the other. Her eyes popped open in surprise, then pure joy. Damn, it was good to see that expression whenever I touched her these days.

The guarded woman who was afraid I had one foot out the door had pretty much vanished. We'd come a long way in such a short time.

"Hi."

I leaned in and touched my lips to hers. "Hi."

"Are you my surprise?"

"Not quite."

"Oh?" She nibbled on her lower lip and I couldn't resist stealing another kiss before moving out of the way. Her brown eyes immediately filled as she caught sight of the car-couch. "Oh, Gage."

"Are those good tears?"

"Yes." She caught my hand and dragged me onto the couch with her. "Oh, it's even comfortable."

"As if I'd make it any other way."

"True. But the coolness factor could easily trump comfort."

"Not if you have to sit in it for two hours straight." I pulled a remote out of my back pocket and aimed it at the tidy screen hidden in the ceiling. It slowly lowered and tipped slightly so we wouldn't have to crane our necks to watch a movie.

She gripped my arm. "No way. You got the screen set up too?"

"I did. There was much swearing as Gideon and Tish figured out how to make it work."

"It's amazing."

"Good. Now sit there and I'll be right back."

She shook her head. "All right."

I crossed the room to the counter where Macy had two bottles of orange soda and the popcorn. She gave me a bowl that was approximately a quarter of the size we usually used for movie nights.

I frowned at her.

"I figure you'll go into cardiac arrest if you have to wait for her to get through the big bowl," she said under her breath.

"You are a genius." I took out the ring box from my pocket and placed the simple oval solitaire in the bottom of the bowl.

"This, I know. Now I'm going to turn out the lights and lock up." Macy held the popcorn back from me. "Do not contaminate my brand-new couch."

"I'll behave." I had leather cleaner in my shop if we didn't anyway.

She narrowed her eyes at me but handed me the popcorn and slapped me on the arm. "Good luck, idiot."

"Thanks." Nerves clawed up my throat as I filled the bowl with Ry's favorite toffee and cheddar popcorn. I took the remainder of the bag, the bowl, and our drinks back to her.

"Macy didn't want to come over?"

"We showed her the couch already."

"Oh." Ry frowned. "And you didn't call me down too?"

I sat down next to her. "I wanted you to see it with just me. Not checking out Macy for her reaction."

"Aww, look at you. All romantic and thoughtful. So sweet." She took a sip of her soda, then leaned over to the other side of the seat. "Man, look at that. There are even cup holders on each side of the car. I can't believe you did all this."

She slid closer to me and I immediately wrapped my arm around her shoulders. "I told you I was going to make it special."

"A car. I can't even. Just...wow. You and Dare did this?"

"And Tish. She made a special frame for the couch. Should have heard her swearing as she figured out how couches are built. She was on Skype with some furniture dude for an hour, figuring it out."

"All this for me?" Ry's eyes filled again.

"I'd do anything for you, huntress. You know that."

She blinked away the tears. "I know, but it's all so amazing."

"And I have ideas for more car couches to make that patio idea of yours even cooler."

"Oh my God, like the drive-ins, only comfortable? An outdoor screen. Oh, it could be so cool!"

"Cool is the word of the night," I said with a laugh. I set the popcorn bowl on her lap.

"What is this? Are we on a diet?" Her eyes narrowed at me.

"No way. I have a huge bag right here." I lifted it off the table beside us.

"Then what's with the little bowl?"

I shrugged. Man, this woman was way too suspicious. "Ask Macy. That's the bowl she gave me."

"Oh." Rylee looked down. "Well, my lap is rapidly disappearing. Maybe she thought I'd knock it on the floor." She tucked it between us and angled herself against my chest. "I'll just have to be careful."

Please don't knock the bowl on the floor.

God, I could just picture her ring disappearing into some bat or pumpkin crowded corner and being forever lost.

I lowered my mouth to hers. "You're perfect."

"Flatterer. What are we watching?"

"I was thinking we should go for *Halloween.*"

"Oh, old school." She dug into the popcorn and munched through a handful as I got the movie set to play. "This is incredible, Gage. Thank you so much for doing this for me. Well, for Macy too."

"Mostly for you." I kissed her again, coming away with the salty taste of her on my lips.

We settled in and I watched her hand more than the damn movie. Good thing I knew it backward and forward.

"You okay?"

"What?"

She rolled her eyes. "You keep staring at me."

"Well, you are way more attractive than Michael."

"Good answer. You're still being weird."

"Popcorn okay?"

"Yeah, why?"

"You're just not eating it as fast as you usually do."

"First, I've got to have a smaller bowl and now I'm not eating it fast enough?" She tossed a kernel at me. "You looking for a fight, buddy?"

"God, no. Just making sure you're comfy and happy."

"Weirdo."

I ate way more of the sweet and salty popcorn that I usually would have. While I enjoyed it, my gut was a damn mess.

The sound of her nails along the bottom of the bowl made me stiffen. Would she finally feel it?

"Looks like we need a refill. Happy now?"

I wanted to bite off my damn tongue. I tipped the bowl a little and she frowned. "If you get popcorn salt on this new couch, Macy will kick your ass. Me too."

"Oh, for God's sake." I tangled my fingers with hers until the ring slid on the tip of her finger.

Her eyes went round as she slowly pulled her hand out of the bowl. "Gage."

"I thought it would be funny and sweet to have you find the damn ring, but now I—"

She lurched at me, her hands cupping my face, the ring tight on her forefinger against my cheek as she kissed me. Her lips salty with her favorite popcorn and a few tears, she wound her arms around my neck and squeezed. "Oh my God." She was looking over my shoulder at her hand. "I can't believe you did this." She slapped my shoulder. "It's so gorgeous. Holy crap, gorgeous."

I wrapped my arms around her. "So, that's a good surprise."

A shriek from the movie made both of us laugh. Michael was stalking some poor girl on the screen. I fumbled for the remote and hit pause, then slid down to the floor.

Ry covered her mouth with the hand she'd hooked the ring onto. It glittered off her forefinger as I grinned up at her. I gently pulled her hand down and slid it off. "Rylee Ford, we pretty much do everything backward in this relationship, but I promise I'll keep you laughing and as happy as I can. I love you more than I thought was possible." I gently cupped her belly. "This little girl or boy may have surprised both of us, but there's nothing I would change." I leaned forward to kiss her belly. "Because this little one gave me you. I didn't even know how much I needed you until you were right in front of me."

"Oh, Gage." Tears ran unchecked down her cheeks. "I love you too. So very much."

"So, that's a yes?"

"You didn't ask yet."

"Oh, right." I laughed and blinked away the sting in my own eyes. "Rylee Ford, will you marry me?"

"Yes. A thousand times yes."

I took her left hand and slid the ring on her finger, then crowded her on the couch and kissed away all her tears, just like I planned on doing for the rest of my life.

Hopefully, we would have more laughter than sorrow. We were off to a damn good start.

Thanks for reading PIT STOP: BABY!
We appreciate our readers so much!
If you loved the book please let your friends know.
If you're so inclined, we'd love a review on your favorite book site.

Every day, Vee makes Moose his coffee. Tonight, he'll deliver the cream.

Turn the page for a special sneak peek of
BABY DADDY WANTED - Crescent Cove Book 5.

BABY DADDY WANTED

MURPHY

Veronica Dixon: BABY DADDY WANTED

Single, personable woman seeking a man for the purposes of procreation. I wouldn't mind if he looks like Chris Pratt, but that's not required. No further interaction with the child is necessary, unless desired by father-to-be. Child will be created the old-fashioned way, assuming both parties agree. Contact V at goodtothelastdrop.

I DROPPED MY PHONE. IT CLATTERED AGAINST MY COFFEE CUP AT THE edge of my makeshift desk and splashed up to soak my work shirt and the sketch paper I was using. "Oh, crap." I stood and stumbled back, knocking into the pail of cement behind me. I quickly yanked off my shirt, swiping at the sticky mess.

"Watch it, Moose."

"Sorry." I turned to steady the pail.

John Gideon, my best friend and pseudo-boss, shook his head with a half grin. "Finally stripping for Mrs. Gunderson?" Suddenly, he winced. "Oh, man. Macy's thermos keeps coffee blistering hot, God bless her."

"Emphasis on the blistering."

"Go splash some water on it before it blisters for real."

"Yeah. Fu—" I swallowed the swear words. This particular client didn't like cussing. She had a comment or opinion on just about everything when it came to the Cove. Unfortunately, she was one of Gideon's best clients. She contracted at least four big projects a year. Personally, I was pretty sure she just liked to have shirtless guys in her backyard—especially Lucky. Though most women hung around to get a look at Lucky, to be honest.

And he liked to be looked at.

I shook off my phone and wiped it against my cargo pants before sliding it in my pocket. "I'm going to go change my shirt. I've got one in the truck."

Gideon nodded. "Go on inside first. We turned off the outside water, remember?"

"Yeah." I didn't want to go inside and have Mrs. Gunderson fuss over me. Or stare at me. I hissed as I wiped at the sugary coffee sticking to my chest hair. Macy at Brewed Awakening knew my weakness. Caramel toffee chocolate coffee. Tasted damn good in the cup, not so much on me.

I resisted the urge to pull out my phone again. I couldn't have read that right. Everyone in Crescent Cove checked the town Facebook page. Lost dog, lost cat, even a lost guinea pig last week. Those, I understood. But Vee posting that?

No way.

I had to be going crazy. Or maybe it was because I just wanted to see her name. It almost didn't compute. She was just Vee to all of us in town. The sweet baker and barista who worked at Brewed Awakening. Huge green eyes and soft blond hair tipped with a rainbow of colors. I never knew what color she'd be sporting when I got my daily dose of caffeine.

She was the highlight of my day.

Always.

"Stupid, Moose," I muttered and pulled my phone out again. Sure enough, there it was. An ad for an honest to God baby daddy. What was she thinking?

"Murphy Masterson, what have you done to yourself?"

I looked up from my phone and shoved it back in my pocket. "Hi, Mrs. Gunderson. I had a little accident with my coffee. Think I could wash up right quick?"

"Of course, come on in." Her bluebell eyes lit. "Can I make you another cup? I know I don't do nearly as well as Macy and Veronica, but I have one of those Keurig machines."

"Don't go to any fuss, ma'am."

"It's no fuss. Speaking of Veronica. What was she thinking posting that on the town group page? It's not a meat market."

I swallowed hard. "I don't know, Mrs. Gunderson." And I was just as surprised. God, had everyone seen it?

"But you did see it."

"It's none of my business."

"You're a good man, Moose. I appreciate that you wouldn't talk about that sweet girl out of turn, but the whole town is talking about it."

How the heck would she know? She'd been here the entire time we were working. Then again, Judy Gunderson could work a phone tree faster than the school snow day listings.

"Do you have a towel?"

"Oh, yes. I'm sorry. I'm just so distracted." She opened a drawer and handed me two plaid towels. "We've been talking about this Veronica thing all morning. I just can't believe it."

Neither could I, but I really didn't want to discuss it with Mrs. Gunderson. I took the towels with strained smile. "I'll just—"

"When you go over there for lunch, you better check on her."

Did everyone know how many times a day I went to Brewed Awakening?

"I brought my lunch."

She clucked her tongue. "You always go over for another coffee. You and John are practically addicted."

I huffed out a breath. "I'll be sure to check on Vee." I hurried down the hall to her bathroom before she could interrogate me any further. I ran the water and splashed it against my chest with a hiss. Her bathroom had been our last remodel. I didn't remember the mirror being quite so big when I'd helped Gideon put it in.

My chest was bright pink under the chest hair that spread across my pecs. What I needed was a shower and a tube of triple antibiotic. "Shit," I mumbled as I did the best I could with the tea towel she'd given me.

But while I had the space to myself, I leaned against the counter and checked my phone again. There were already eleven comments on her post and a dozen likes, hearts, and many shocked faces. Not a single reply from Vee herself though.

Had she really meant to post that to the group's main page?

She wasn't exactly the type to put all her business on Facebook, but then again, she wasn't quiet about giving her opinions. Especially when she and Macy got going. They were entertaining as hell, and I wished I had the balls to act on my feelings for her.

But to post this? It just didn't make sense.

Before I could stop myself, I messaged her using my business account. I just needed to check on her and make sure she meant to post it. That was all.

Now Available

For more information go to www.tarynquinn.com

CRESCENT COVE CHARACTER CHART

BEWARE...SPOILERS APLENTY IN THIS CHARACTER CHART. READ AT YOUR OWN RISK!

Ally Lawrence:
Married to Seth Hamilton, mother to Alexander, stepmother to Laurie, best friends with Sage Evans

Andrea Maria Fortuna Dixon Newman:
Mother to Veronica 'Vee' Dixon

Asher Wainwright: CEO Wainwright Publishing
Involved with Hannah Jacobs, father to Lily and Rose

August Beck: Owns Beck Furniture
Brother to Caleb and Ivy, involved with Kinleigh Scott

Beckett Manning: Owns Happy Acres Orchard
Brother to Zoe, Hayes, and Justin

Bess Wainwright:
Grandmother to Asher Wainwright

Caleb Beck: Teaches second grade

Brother to August and Ivy

(Charles) Dare Kramer: Mechanic, owns J & T Body Shop
Married to Kelsey Ford, son Weston (mother is Katherine), son Sean, brother Gage

Christian Masterson: Sheriff's Deputy
Brother to Murphy, Travis, and Penn, sister Madison 'Maddie'

Cindy Ford:
Married to Doug Ford, mother of Kelsey and Rylee

Dahlia McKenna: Designer/Decorator who works with Macy

Damien Ramos:
Sisters Erica, Francesca, Gabriela, Regina

Doug Ford:
Married to Cindy Ford, father of Kelsey and Rylee Ford

Gavin Forrester: Real estate owner

Gabriela 'Gabby' Ramos:
Brother Damien, sisters Erica, Francesca, Regina, best friend Hannah Jacobs

Greta: Manager of the Rusty Spoon

Hank Masterson:
Married to JoAnn Masterson, sons Murphy, Christian, Travis, Penn, and daughter Madison

Hannah Jacobs:
Involved with Asher Wainwright, mother to Lily and Rose, best friend Gabriela Ramos

Hayes Manning: Owns Happy Acres Orchard
Brother to Zoe, Beckett, and Justin

Ian Kagan: Solo artist
Brother to Simon, engaged to Zoe Manning, son Elvis, best friend Rory Ferguson, friends with Flynn Sheppard and Kellan McGuire

Ivy Beck: Waitress at the Rusty Spoon and owns Rolling Cones ice cream truck
Sister to Caleb and August, engaged to Rory Ferguson, best friend Kinleigh Scott, friends with Maggie Kelly and Zoe Manning

James Hamilton: Owns Hamilton Realty
Father to Seth and Oliver Hamilton

Jared Brooks: Sheriff
Brother to Mason Brooks, best friend Gina Ramos

Jessica Gideon: Famous actress
Ex-wife to John Gideon, mother to Dani

JoAnn Masterson:
Married to Hank Masterson, sons Murphy, Christian, Travis, Penn, and daughter Madison

John Gideon: Owns Gideon Gets it Done Handyman Service
Daughter Dani, ex-wife Jessica Gideon

Justin Manning: Owns Happy Acres Orchard
Brother to Zoe, Beckett, and Hayes

Kellan McGuire: Lead singer Wilder Mind, solo artist
Brother to Bethany, married to Maggie Kelly, son Wolf, friends with Rory Ferguson, Ian Kagan, and Myles Vaughn

Kelsey Ford: Elementary school teacher
Married to Dare Kramer, son Sean, stepson Weston, sister Rylee Ford

Kinleigh Scott: Owns Kinleigh's
Cousin Vincent Scott, best friend Ivy Beck, involved with August Beck

(Lucas) Gage Kramer: Owns J & T Body Shop, former race car driver
Married to Rylee Ford, daughter Hayley Kramer, brother Dare Kramer

Lucky Roberts: Works for Gideon Gets it Done Handyman Service

Macy Devereaux: Owns Brewed Awakening and The Haunt
Sister to Nolan, best friend Rylee Ford

Madison 'Maddie' Masterson:
Sister to Murphy, Christian, Travis, and Penn

Marjorie Hamilton:
Ex-wife of Seth Hamilton, birth mother of Laurie Hamilton

Mason Brooks: Owns Mason Jar restaurant
Brother Jared Brooks

Maggie Kelly:
Married to Kellan McGuire, son Wolf, best friend Kendra Russo, friends with Ivy Beck and Zoe Manning

Melissa Kramer: Owns Robbie's Pizza
Married to Robert Kramer, mother of Dare and Gage Kramer

Mike London: High school teacher

Mitch Cooper: Owns the Rusty Spoon

Murphy 'Moose' Masterson: Game Designer/Construction Contractor and Owns Baby Daddy Wanted
Married to Vee Dixon, son Brayden, brother to Christian, Travis, Penn, and Maddie

Nolan Devereaux: Owns Tricks and Treats Candy Shop
Brother to Macy

Oliver Hamilton: Owns Hamilton Realty and the Hummingbird's Nest
Married to Sage Evans, daughter Star, twin brother Seth Hamilton

Penn Masterson: Graphic novelist
Brother to Murphy, Travis, Christian, and Maddie

Regina 'Gina' Ramos: Waitress at the Rusty Spoon
Brother Damien, sisters Erica, Francesca, Gabriela, best friend Sheriff Brooks

Robert Kramer: Owns Robbie's Pizza
Married to Melissa Kramer, father of Dare and Gage Kramer

Rory Ferguson: Record Producer/Rhythm Guitarist
Brother to Thomas and Maureen, engaged to Ivy Beck, best friend Ian Kagan, friends with Flynn Sheppard and Kellan McGuire

Rylee Ford: Barista at Brewed Awakening
Married to Gage Kramer, daughter Hayley, sister Kelsey Ford Kramer, best friend Macy Devereaux

Sage Evans: Owns the Hummingbird's Nest
Married to Oliver Hamilton, daughter Star, best friend Ally Lawrence

Seth Hamilton: Owns Hamilton Realty

Married to Ally Lawrence, daughter Laurie, son Alexander, twin brother to Oliver Hamilton, ex-wife Marjorie

Tish Burns: Owns J & T Body Shop, custom fabricator
Friends with Gage Kramer

Travis Masterson:
Brothers Christian, Penn and Murphy, and Maddie, daughter Carrington

Veronica 'Vee' Dixon: Pastry Baker, owns Baby Daddy Wanted
Married to Murphy Masterson, son Brayden

Vincent Scott: partner in Wainwright Publishing Industries
Cousin Kinleigh Scott

Zoe Manning: Artist/photographer
Sister to Beckett, Hayes, and Justin, engaged to Ian Kagan, son Elvis, cousin Lila Ronson Shawcross Crandall, friends with Ivy Beck and Maggie Kelly

*AS OF 10/30/19

Have My Baby

Claim My Baby

Who's The Daddy

Pit Stop: Baby

Baby Daddy Wanted

Rockstar Baby

Daddy in Disguise

My Ex's Baby

Daddy Undercover

Crescent Cove Standalones

CEO Daddy

Stand-in Daddy

ALSO BY TARYN QUINN

Afternoon Delight

Dirty Distractions

Drawn Deep

Deuces Wild

Protecting His Rockstar

Guarding His Best Friend's Sister

Shielding His Baby

Wilder Rock

Rockstar Daddy

Holiday Books

Unwrapped

Holiday Sparks

Filthy Scrooge

Jingle Ball

Bad Kitty

For more information about our books visit

www.tarynquinn.com

ABOUT TARYN QUINN

USA Today bestselling author, ***Taryn Quinn,*** is the redheaded stepchild of bestselling authors Taryn Elliott & Cari Quinn. We've been writing together for a lifetime—wait, no it's really been only a handful of years, but we have a lot of fun. Sometimes we write stories that don't quite fit into our regular catalog.

* Ultra sexy—check.
* Quirky characters—check.
* Sweet–usually mixed in with the sexy...so, yeah—check.
* RomCom—check.
* Dark and twisted—check.

A little something for everyone.

So, c'mon in. Light some candles, pour a glass of wine...maybe even put on some sexy music.

For more information about us...

tarynquinn.com

tq@tarynquinn.com

QUINN AND ELLIOTT

We also write more serious, longer, and sexier books as Cari Quinn & Taryn Elliott. Our topics include mostly rockstars, but mobsters, MMA, and a little suspense gets tossed in there too.

Rockers' Series Reading Order

Lost in Oblivion

Winchester Falls

Found in Oblivion

Hammered

Rock Revenge

Brooklyn Dawn

Other Series

The Boss

Tapped Out

Love Required

Boys of Fall

If you'd like more information about us please visit

www.quinnandelliott.com

Made in the USA
Coppell, TX
31 October 2022